Letters to My Dad
Diary of a Preborn Daughter

JOEL PATCHEN

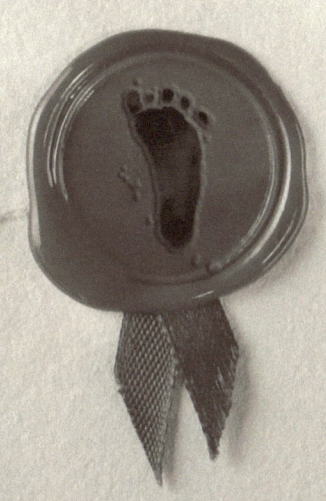

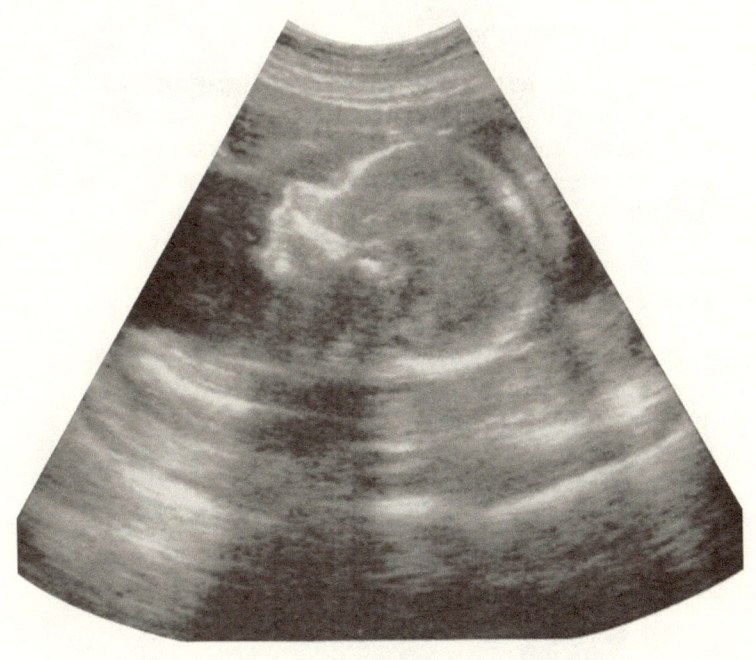

If you are interested in the medical discoveries regarding embryonic and fetal life and the biblical support for the narrative, please read the notes at the close of the book and their corresponding diary dates.

Letters to My Dad

© 2011 Joel Patchen

Second Edition.
Previously titled: Brooke Anna: Letters from a Preborn Girl

Scripture taken from the NEW AMERICAN STANDARD BIBLE®, copyright © 1960, 1962, 1963, 1968, 1971, 1972, 1973, 1975, 1977, 1995, by The Lockman Foundation. Used by permission.

Also referenced: The Holy Bible, NEW AMERICAN STANDARD BIBLE, COMPACT REFERENCE BIBLE (NASB®). Grand Rapids, Michigan: Zondervan Publishing, 2000.

Published by Anna's Choice, LLC
Colorado Springs, Colorado
www.annaschoice.org
ISBN 978-0-9818870-5-0
Cover and interior design: Granite Creative, inc.
Editorial assistance: GoodEditors.com
Printed in the United States of America

Dedicated
To The Human Race

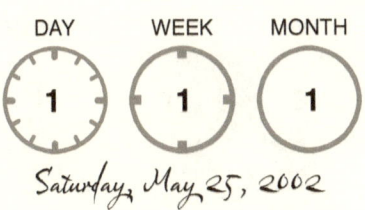

Saturday, May 25, 2002

Dear Daddy,

    Today I was created by God! I cannot articulate my creation adequately, but it was as if in a flash of light all the colors of the spectrum shown forth, and I knew I existed, my body imperceptible, as my newly formed DNA teemed with life. Although I could not yet move in all my fullness, my soul felt its worth as my genes worked feverishly to reveal the beauty that is me. I think every person God creates must be beautiful. How could anyone fashioned by His grand hands be anything less? Yesterday I was known only to God, but today I'm known to myself and God.

    I feel privileged to be writing to you about my life in the womb. Mommy will be the first to feel me, but I want you to know my mind's intimate counsel and my soul's secrets. Cherish this diary, Daddy—I'm not quite sure the purpose it will serve, but I sense it is something important and worthy of writing. Today, no doubt, you are oblivious to my presence and existence, but I want you to know that I'm overwhelmed by life and the joy of being. I look forward to meeting you in the future, but for now I must rest. I sense there is much work to be done!

Thursday, May 30, 2002

Dear Daddy,

My cellular growth has been intense, exhausting, and exhilarating. The adrenaline of creation is amazing. I wonder if anything in my life going forward will match this productivity and excitement! Each moment is filled with newness, achievement, and grandeur. It's as if I'm copying myself a hundred times, but each new version has a different mission or purpose. I can't imagine what I will experience upon completion of my development, but I think no work of art could compare with me. God's work is wonderful, and I feel His pleasure as I am being fashioned in His presence. I'm grateful to God for allowing me to write this diary through His supernatural power, for without it this would never be possible, and I might come to forget the miracle that transpired here and its profound impression on a girl not yet a week old.

Daddy, did I mention I'm traveling? I'm not sure exactly where I'm going, but I sense it's going to be a beautiful temple of preparation—a sanctuary of peace and safety. Whatever the destination, I'm enjoying the journey. Do you remember your first days of life? I'm sure you, too, must have a wonderful story of beginning and new life. Oh, Daddy, I'm so happy to be alive! I can't wait to experience tomorrow and feel the joy it will bring. Got to go. I feel something amazing is about to happen.

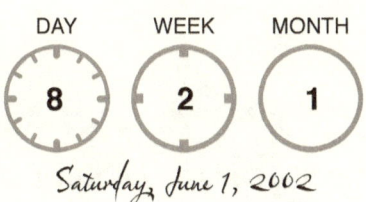

Saturday, June 1, 2002

Dear Daddy,

My day started abruptly as I slammed into what felt like a very sturdy wall. I was taken by surprise and jostled about from the impact. But after an initial friction, I felt as if I was being cuddled in a warm, soft blanket. It was an overwhelming sensation of comfort and trust. I gave myself wholly to the experience and reveled in the bliss for what seemed like days—the sheer height of ecstasy. Where I had been before was nice, but this was sublime. I knew for the first time what it felt like to be part of a home—part of a family! I could feel Mommy's presence, and I knew she was strong and capable of protecting me. Joy flooded over me as I realized she was made for this very purpose and by the same hands that were fashioning me. I wonder what she's like. Is she tall? Pretty? Gentle and caring? Funny or serious? Intellectual or imaginative? Does she have a dark or light complexion? What is her age? Does she sense I'm alive, or can she even guess at the miracle taking place inside her womb?

As I contemplated the mystery of Mommy, I began to imagine my own mysteries. Would I be like my mother or my father, a combination of the two, or something altogether different? Would I be tall or pretty? I began to marvel at all the discoveries that awaited me and all the things I would learn and experience along

3

this journey of life. Daddy, I can't wait for tomorrow! Surely, it will be filled with amazing joys and things too wonderful for me to know.

One last thing, Daddy: When you read this diary, please tell Mommy I love her and that I'm grateful for everything she's done for me. I'm so blessed to have her for my mother. I know God chose her for me!

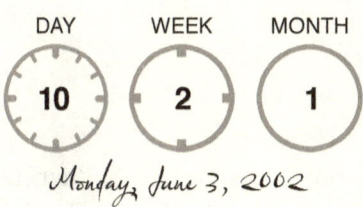

DAY   WEEK   MONTH

10   2   1

Monday, June 3, 2002

Dear Daddy,

Today I am ten days old! An achievement, I feel, worthy of noting and celebrating. I have barely been able to catch my breath the last few days as I have been busy producing an important hormone God showed me how to release. Daddy, God explained that a hormone is something special He created that stimulates the growth of my cells. This key hormone will set the stage for my nourishment over the next nine months. He said it was called *human chorionic gonadotrophin.* It tells Mommy's body to continue to produce another hormone called *progesterone* and suppress her normal cycle. I confess I have no idea what God is talking about, but I've followed His instructions to the letter as I'm confident He knows what He's doing. Even as God does the lion's share of the work, it seems His plan is to involve me in the process and teach me things. One thing I've learned during this hormone's production is the joy of accomplishment and the sweetness of rest after a job well done. It seems God has designed me for work and fellowship, and I like that. He's even started calling me by my name: Brooke.

Do you like to work, Daddy? I bet you do, especially when it's worth doing or it's something you love. Does Mommy work, too? When I grow up, I want to do something noble and important. Something you and God would be proud of. Maybe I will build or design

things like God. He is a great builder, fashioning my body with His own hands. Perhaps I will be an accomplished writer. God said, "My child, I've written My truth in the heavens." Better yet, maybe I'll work with people. God told me, "Brooke, I love every person I create. People are the object of My affection—worth dying for." Whatever I do, I'm sure it will be grand.

It's impossible for me to describe all that goes on in my cells or in Mommy's womb without God's direction and supernatural power. I truly have a front-row seat to the miraculous! I'm astonished and perplexed by all that occurs within and around me. Each day I grow bigger and more capable. Often I feel as if I'm going to burst from all the activity and excitement. God is so marvelously good to me, Daddy. I hope you're having a wonderful time reading this account of my life. I'm having a great time writing it.

Yours, Brooke

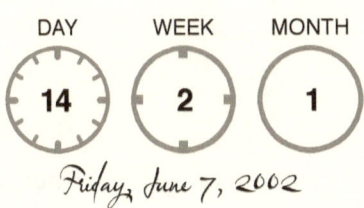

Friday, June 7, 2002

Dear Daddy,

Today as I awoke from my sleep, I heard the sound of rushing water as the voice of the Lord spoke to my cells. His words began an amazing process by which my substance began to form into different layers, or maybe "bubbles" is a better word. After a convulsive but contained shock, I asked Him what He was doing, and He said, "My child, I'm laying the groundwork for your central nervous system and your organ formation." As I grappled with this revelation, a stillness filled my conscience. All was quiet, like a great void, and then in a moment, like a flash of lightning, I felt a tremendous surge, and I began to tingle. I felt my surroundings in a whole new way and to an entirely different degree. I would have been overcome by fear if it were not for the comforting words of God. He is an intimidating force at times, but His gentleness and care calms my soul. Oh, Daddy, what will I become? Who shall I be? I can only guess that I must have a glorious purpose, for why else would this most magnificent God create me?

I like this new sensitivity to the things around me. It gives me more to process and discern. Being able to feel things better than before makes me feel so alive, so interactive. I love that God, in His goodness, has granted me independence even in the midst of my great dependence on Him. I marvel at His design of my body and His plan to use Mommy as a shield and a source for

nutrition and shelter. I feel so safe in her womb. I don't know what I would do without her. I sense I'll always have a special bond with her. It's like we were made for each other. I'm grateful that God has allowed us to be in relationship from the very beginning.

Daddy, I know Mommy protects me, but who protects Mommy? Do you? Does she feel as safe and cared for by you as I do by her? I hope so, Daddy. Please take good care of Mommy and me. Surely God must watch over all of us—He is so strong and capable. When He speaks to me, I feel as if nothing could snatch me from His hand. It's easy to feel secure in God's presence.

Sorry, Daddy, but I've got to stop writing now. The activities of the day have exhausted me, and I can feel my energy draining. I'll write again soon.

Yours, Brooke

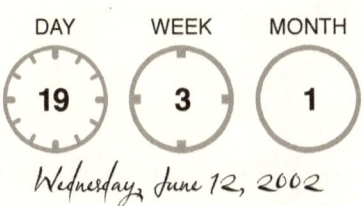

Wednesday, June 12, 2002

Dear Daddy,

Sorry I haven't written sooner, but each day has been a whirlwind of activity, formation, and growth. I'm so small I doubt anybody could see me, but I'm a full-fledged factory—one that has begun production of my spinal cord, brain, and blood vessels. While each of these complex systems will take on more specific duties as I continue to grow, their foundation has already been laid. God has entrusted me with the blueprints for their completion, and I have developed all the tools necessary for their intricate construction over time.

I know it's a big responsibility, but God has faith in me. He said, "Brooke, I will never leave you, I'll be right beside you every step of the way." It's comforting to know that if I have questions or problems, all I need to do is call upon Him. Besides, the directions He gave me are so detailed and easy to understand that I don't know how I could mess things up. With His guidance, I know I will make the right decisions. It makes me feel good to know that God trusts and values me. It's wonderful that He has chosen to include me in this process.

When I think about it, God has allowed all of us to play a part in this miracle of me. You, Mommy, and me, we've all played a role in this journey. God must have a great adventure and purpose planned for each of us, a special destiny only we can fulfill. I know you must

believe this, too. Just think of it—you protect Mommy and me, Mommy provides all the supplies I need, and I do the rest (just kidding, Daddy)! I know it's a team effort. God even told me that you got to play a role in determining my gender. How cool is that! I hope I live up to your expectations of what a daughter can be—that I'll be the kind of daughter you always wanted.

Before I stop writing, I must tell you one last thing. Even though my brain is just beginning to form, it is the most awesome thing God has done so far. Its capacity and capabilities seem endless. My level of self-aware-ness and understanding has improved tremendously. My brain is like a high-powered engine just waiting for a body to drive. I know it's going to be super helpful in the days to come.

Yours, Brooke

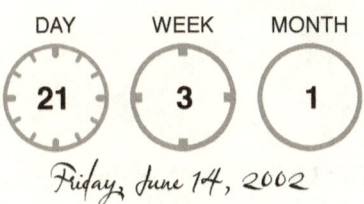

Friday, June 14, 2002

Dear Daddy,

I'm beat—exhausted! All these new connections, cells, and body systems I improve and form every day can sap one's strength. For example, as my nerves extend and report new information to my brain, the speed is remarkable. The pace must be several hundred miles an hour—causing me to expend great energy. I wouldn't be able to keep up with the demand for production if it weren't for the mystical power of God. Within the multitude of my tasks, it seems as if He bends time. In the rush of activity, moments of incredible slowness will develop, and what seemingly takes days or months to complete is really only a matter of seconds. My incomplete brain's ability to multitask is phenomenal! I'm in awe of the complex genes, chemicals, and systems required to direct my growth and development. I'm a puzzle to myself, and I have the blueprints. Daddy, I'm not just a witness to the miraculous—I am a miracle!

Even though things are going well, I'm a little concerned about my lack of energy. I've begun to feel my limitations, and if something doesn't change, I don't know how I'll keep up with production. Something is missing. God seems undeterred and just says that I need to trust Him. But I worry something is wrong. Is there something He's not telling me? He's never failed me or lied to me. Still, I can't escape these feelings and completely trust Him.

I told God I felt uncomfortable and uneasy, and He said, "My child, what you're feeling is called *fear*, and you must overcome it. The way to overcome fear is by placing your faith in Me!" When I asked Him what faith was, He said, "Faith is the assurance of things hoped for and the conviction of things not seen" (which went a little over my head). And then He said, "Just trust in Me."

Do you have faith, Daddy? Is it hard for you to trust God? I'll bet at your age you don't have these problems. Anyway, I'm going to give it a try and place my faith in God to supply the energy I need.

Yours, Brooke

Sunday, June 16, 2002

Dear Daddy,

Wow, what a day today has been! Yesterday, I worked all day making cells, laying down blood vessels, and fighting fatigue. God gave me the important job of making clusters of *mesoderm* cells, which He said would form vital pathways for blood distribution in my body. I worked hard, and whenever I felt I couldn't go any longer, I cried out and said, "Give me faith, I trust in You." As soon as the words left me, I would receive a pulse of energy and be able to continue my task.

About midday, while I was still busy working, I felt God's warm hands at work in the center of my being. He was forming a clump of cells in a squiggly shape— sort of like the letter S. As He worked, great heat was generated and released in a cloudless vapor. After a rush of energy and connection, He spoke. At the breath of His mouth, I felt a surge so indescribably strong that I worried I might explode. And then out of my gasp, I heard a beat, low and powerful, and my whole being surged with energy and vitality! When I gathered myself from the shock, I asked Him, "What was that?" He responded with these words, "I've just formed your heart, little one."

Oh, Daddy, it's marvelous—now I see the power of faith and the goodness of God! A few days ago I thought my brain was an engine, but I see now I was

wrong. Nothing can match the power of my heart. My brain is the control room, but my heart is a reactor. A power plant connected to my soul. With the gifts of my brain and my heart, I know I can complete whatever remaining tasks God has for me.

Rejoice with me, Daddy. I'm so amazed by God's provision and His care for me. I feel different today! It's as if somehow I belong to a greater family or group, as if I'm part of something beyond myself . . . part of a community . . . and I share a fellowship with all humankind. What a journey this has been! Celebrate today with me, Daddy. I'll never forget it. Here in this moment, my hopes have been realized, and I'm certain my unseen heart has all it needs for life and love.

Yours affectionately, Brooke

DAY   WEEK   MONTH

28   **4**   **1**

Friday, June 21, 2002

Dear Daddy,

    My strong heart has increased production in every area of my body. I've started to work on my digestive tract (which includes a stomach, gall bladder, pancreas, and liver), arms, legs, eyes, and ears. My blood is beginning to propel through my body and provide the nutrients and oxygen necessary to sustain life. My heart beats at least eighty times a minute, and it's on the increase. Before I paused to write this entry, I began construction of my lungs and my reproductive germ cells. It's totally awesome, Daddy. The power to develop that God has placed at my disposal is unfathomable. There's no stopping this process, and I know I will become what God has fashioned me to be.

    The blueprints I'm using to develop my organs are pure genius. The way they function and harmonize, only God could have made such plans. I can't wait to realize their potential and see what I can do upon completion. I can only guess at all the things I will be able to experience. Oh, the wonders that await discovery! Even in the midst of my work and the newness of each day, I sometimes get impatient for the future and all the glories it must hold. I think about being known to you and Mommy the way I'm known to God. I think about speaking to you, laughing with you, and enjoying

you. How long must I wait to be with you? Daddy, I'm coming; wait for me. Soon, we can hold hands and walk through this life together!

Well, enough daydreaming. I must get back to the never-ending projects before me.

Yours, Brooke

Tuesday, July 2, 2002

Dear Daddy,

I was thinking today about Mommy and what it's like to be a mother—to have a daughter to love, teach, and be with. It must be a great feeling and privilege to be a mother—to have a child of your own flesh. Is your mother still an important part of your life, Daddy? Do you still do things together and share in the fun of being? I hope so. What joy must be yours to be part of a family and enjoy the kindred fellowship of common blood. I feel very fortunate to be a part of our family, even if I'm not noticed yet. I know someday soon I will be.

I'm still growing at a rapid pace. You should see me. Everything is getting bigger and better with each day's work. God has been a tremendous help to me. I feel His presence guiding me when I get off track or start to go in the wrong direction. He always brings me back to the right path and keeps me focused on the assignment He's given me. He's so comforting and good. I hope you're like Him—it would be a shame if you're not. Don't worry, I won't expect you to be all that God is, but I hope He's taught you some of the things He's teaching me. Wouldn't it be great if we both knew Him equally well?

I know tomorrow is going to be another busy day, so I better cut this communication short and shut down for a little while. I'm thinking of you and knowing when we meet, it will be grand.

Yours, Brooke

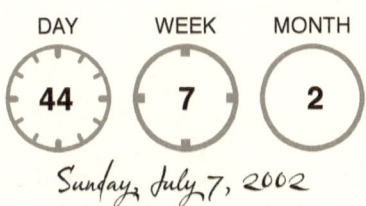

Sunday, July 7, 2002

Dear Daddy,

I'm past six weeks old and huge compared to when I started growing. I asked God to help me give you a reference point for my current size, and He said, "Tell him you're about the size of a kidney bean." Which I'm assuming is pretty small to you, but is, nonetheless, a good description of me at this point. My arms and legs have started to extend from my body, and I'm beginning to develop hands and feet. My brain, heart, eyes, and ears continue to develop and expand their capabilities and function. With each passing moment, I become more self-sufficient, aware, and specialized. My liver is producing blood cells efficiently, and my kidneys are going through several cycles of development and replacement. I'm delighted with the results of my formation and am looking forward to the full potential of this awesome body God is helping me build.

Something else I want to tell you—I've started to move! It's the most amazing feeling. It's really nothing more than a twitch in my mass or limbs, but it's such a revelation of potential after weeks of what seemed like suspended stillness. My soul, complete at day one, has always been ahead of my mind and body, and to see the beginnings of the things I've sensed all along coming to fruition is pure joy! I can't wait to run and leap and

play. What's it like to move in your full capacity? How breathtaking it will be to think and do without limitation or hesitation. I'm so excited for the days ahead.

I'm loving this time of development. I'm so grateful to God that He chose to make me and give me the opportunity to live—to see the unseen and to know the unknown. The discoveries that await me boggle the mind. Sometimes, I can't contain the joy of life. It wells up inside my soul and makes me giddy, and I feel my body twitch. Oh, the glorious bliss of life!

Yours, Brooke

DAY   WEEK   MONTH

47   7   2

Wednesday, July 10, 2002

Dear Daddy,

Do you sense that I am here? I think Mommy has discovered me. Yesterday, I could feel the warmth of her hands coming from outside this sanctuary of protection she has provided. I could sense she knew about me. I don't know what she was doing, but it had a rhythm and a melody. I felt her sway, and there was something in her movements that bespoke of dreams fulfilled and sublime satisfaction. It made me want to burst in anticipation of being in her loving arms. She loves me, Daddy! I know it! I know it! I can't wait to be with her—to share my love and appreciation for her.

Maybe she's told you about me. I hope so. It would be great for you both to know I exist. Then you could share my joy and your joy could be complete, even if we can't communicate right away. I'm so happy God chose you and Mommy to be my parents. It's just another of His many gifts to me. Daddy, your daughter is here. Can you hear me?

Perhaps God will communicate to your spirit that you have been blessed with a daughter. It feels good to be acknowledged—to be recognized and cherished. I love you, Mommy. I love you, Daddy. Please celebrate

me, as I celebrate you. Until that day when we meet face to face, know that I'm looking forward to the fellowship of family.

Love, Brooke

Saturday, July 13, 2002

Dear Daddy,

What is Mommy doing today? Something different must be going on because I'm fighting to stay awake and the sensations coming from outside my place of preparation are changing noticeably. It's sort of like going in and out of consciousness with noticeable temperature fluctuations. When the temperature is colder, I perceive a rhythm and a repetitive motion that makes me fade out and struggle to stay awake. It seems, however, about the time I give in to this pattern of motion, it stops, and I notice a total lack of undulation. Sway is replaced by stillness and increased warmth. The sensation is delightful, and it makes me want to stretch and luxuriate. Eventually though, it makes me very tired, and the fight to resist sleep begins anew. All in all, it's an amusing, yet frustrating, experience because I don't know what is taking place or happening to Mommy. I suppose I will just have to wait until I'm outside her womb to understand this mystery.

Daddy, I believe by now you must know about me and my presence inside Mommy. But could you even guess that I'm aware of you and am writing to you in this diary? How fun it is to prepare this account for you in secret, to treasure in my heart the day it will be revealed and known. I delight in making you aware of all that is happening with me, your daughter.

I'm still quite busy making things and developing new connections in my body. I've made hundreds of different types of cells, and my hands and feet can almost touch together. One of the most exciting recent developments is what God is doing with my eyes. He has created light-sensitive cells in the retinas, which I understand means "the sensory membrane that lines my eyes." Just yesterday, He finished connecting my retinas to my brain through awesome and powerful nerve connections. The sensations are indescribable. I can't wait to see as you do, Daddy, and experience the joys of perception and information. God told me He soon would be sealing my eyes shut to work on the minute details of this marvel of complexity He calls "the lamp of the body." I must admit it's pure agony to contemplate the weeks of waiting necessary to complete my beautiful eyes. It's torture. But God in His goodness has not left me in the dark. Rather, He has given me the ability to see through the Spirit. It's an unbelievable thing to witness myself being delicately, fearfully, and powerfully made! I am a marvel, Daddy, and I know these words don't even begin to describe what's transpired here. Thanks for listening, Daddy. I have to go.

Yours, Brooke

DAY WEEK MONTH

55 8 2

Thursday, July 18, 2002

Dear Daddy,

I'm rapidly approaching my ninth week of life. The transformation in my body is extraordinary. All my body's systems and organs are now in place and are developing nicely into an integrated unit. My intestines are growing so fast it's incredible. Every day is miracle upon miracle! God suggested I provide you with the following analogy. He said, "Brooke, tell him it's like spending the day at the racetrack—the speed and precision can't be appreciated unless you have a front-row seat." There's also much work to be done in the construction of my highly developed skeletal system. God and I have begun production on several cartilage and bone components. It seems with each passing hour, I become sturdier, stronger, and more capable.

One development, in particular, that I'm excited about is the creation of my tongue and taste buds. These completed parts have opened up a whole new world of sensations and experiences. I'm now able to distinguish more clearly changes in the fluid in which I reside, a new ability that is both perplexing and delightful. It seems as though the complex system for nutrient transmission that God has designed is also improving. My ability to receive food, oxygen, and water from the membrane-like system between Mommy's blood and my own is exquisite. God's handiwork is as mysterious as it is captivating.

As a result of abundant nutrient availability, I've increased my nutrient consumption. This rise in fuel has allowed me to ramp up production and work at optimal levels for extended periods. Recently, I've put this newfound energy to good use—I've spent much time this week connecting and integrating my muscles and nervous system, which has unleashed the ability to move more precisely and purposefully. I find my improved body movement greatly amusing. I love the joy and freedom! Each day is so full of wonder, discovery, and attainment that I barely have time to write in this diary. I'm doing well if I can record my thoughts and experiences once or twice a week. Still, amid the busyness, I'm having the time of my life. Thank You, God, for life! It's great to be alive.

Yours, Brooke

DAY	WEEK	MONTH
58	9	2

Sunday, July 21, 2002

Dear Daddy,

Yesterday was a frightening, illuminating, and powerful day. It started out with alarm, as I noticed for the first time all the cells in my body that die every day and cease to function. Fear crept over me as I contemplated the state of my condition. Were things out of balance? Was I failing to develop properly? As I sought for answers, I became increasingly uneasy and nervous. With each passing moment, I became more and more disturbed until I was lost in a full-fledged internal panic.

Thankfully, God, sensing my worry and discomfort, asked what was bothering me. He listened patiently while I disclosed my new dilemma, and He said, "My child, do you trust Me?"

"I do," I replied.

He then responded, "Brooke, one of My specialties is bringing life out of death!" He went on to explain how He uses the death of cells after they have completed their mission to form and sculpt new life. He orchestrates the balance between living cells and dying cells to formulate and form the intricacies of the body and brain. Nothing is out of balance or wasted. It is all part of His master plan. Though I'm not sure I understood all of what He shared, the peace and comfort I felt as I realized afresh the beauty of His plan was breathtaking. It's incredible to feel His power and contemplate His

care. I felt invincible after our time together. With God on my side, what can harm me? Who can stand against me? After God set me free from my fear, I wanted to dance for joy!

I hope this experience will help me remember I can trust God to calm my fears and provide me with answers to my concerns. May this diary remind me that all I need to do when I'm worried or afraid is to communicate with God and ask Him for help, understanding, or guidance. God has left nothing to chance concerning me. He is developing my soul, mind, and body, equally and completely.

What a fearful and glorious experience yesterday was. My body tingles as I record the event for you and reflect upon the still-fresh memory.

Yours, Brooke

DAY   WEEK   MONTH

60   9   3

Tuesday, July 23, 2002

Dear Daddy,

I've solved the mystery of Mommy's movements from the other day. Today Mommy's movements started out in much the same way as before, with a feeling of cool and then a jostling or undulating motion. I fought even harder this time to resist the desire to doze off, and I realized that the sensation was rhythmic with short pauses followed by a return to the same pattern. After what seemed like a long period of time, the warmth would come, as before, coupled with a blissful stillness. After much thought and deliberation, I realized that Mommy was involved in a consistent activity. But no matter how hard I tried, the type of activity escaped me. So like a smart little girl, I tapped into my resources and asked God to tell me what Mommy was doing. After a short Q&A session that seemed to amuse Him, He said, "My child, the activity you have perceptively discerned is called swimming." As He painted a picture with words about this joyful activity called swimming, I thought about how fun it must be to be living outside the womb. What fun you, me, and Mommy will have when I arrive!

My current setup is not without its joys, however. My ever-improving ability to move has led to greater and greater fun. I, too, can enjoy the boundless wonder of play and the feeling of buoyancy and weightlessness as I move about in the womb. I hope I haven't given

you the impression that it's all work and no play in here, because I do take time to relax and have fun. I love my leisure time. My body and mind are so energized when I play—it truly is a wonderful thing.

Well, Daddy, all the intrigue and discussion of Mommy's swimming activities have left me spent. I desperately needed the naptime I missed. My stubborn determination has led to an overwhelming drowsiness, and I must take my rest. Sending my love and thinking about you.

Yours, Brooke

DAY	WEEK	MONTH
66	10	3

Monday, July 29, 2002

Dear Daddy,

Do you ever feel overwhelmed or overloaded? Sometimes it's all I can do to keep up with the tasks before me. As I pondered what God said about swimming and other things He's shared with me about life outside this place of beginning, I realized just how big and full your world is. It's daunting to think of all the information, opportunities, experiences, and challenges that await me after my days of preparation are complete.

How do you handle it all? Are you ever overcome by the choices and tasks before you, or do you learn to process and filter them? I should think you're never bored with all the wonder and brilliance God has woven into the world. As my mind advances and my soul deepens, I find I can become clouded and frozen. The many thoughts and activities laid before me keep me suspended and of little use. Sometimes it's hard to focus and stay true to what I'm doing. Frustrating! I was going to ask God about it, but I can't seem to locate Him at the moment. He must be off doing something important, or perhaps I haven't looked hard enough for Him. Since you can't help me yet and I can't find God, I'll just have to wait.

It's hard to wait for things, isn't it? To be patient, to trust God. I suppose it requires faith and maturity, two things I'm learning about and working on. As

complex as the construction of my body systems can be at times, I find the development of my mind is even more so. Perhaps that's why God gives us this time in the womb—to develop all aspects of our person so we are complete, not lacking in anything.

Well, enough of my ponderings. Did I mention that I'm around ten weeks old? Very impressive, I know! I'm so pleased with how things are coming along—I'm really taking shape and looking good, if I do say so myself. I wonder if you would recognize me if you saw me inside the womb? If it were possible to see me in a picture, or by opening the womb, could you notice me? Would you brag on me and say, "That's my girl?" I would like to see you, and I suppose, one day soon, I will. Yet another thing I must wait for! I bet for both of us it will be worth the wait.

Before I go, I'll leave you with this tantalizing detail: My external ears are taking shape, very cute and petite. I cannot, as yet, use them to their full capacity, but the allure of their potential is exciting. As always, something to wait for, joyfully!

Yours, Brooke

DAY	WEEK	MONTH
70	10	3

Friday, August 2, 2002

Dear Daddy,

I'm almost 2½ inches long! I'm getting taller, and it is very exciting. Soon I will be as big as you are! Well, someday. Something else I'm thrilled about is my fingers. I just love my long fingers and all the new things they allow me to do. I can tell they are going to be wonderful tools throughout my life. Currently, they're especially great because my fingernails are starting to develop. The nails add such beauty and definition to my fingers. God said I'm not the first woman to notice these fetching additions to the finger. What can I say—God knows how to accessorize.

I've done a better job this week of staying focused and keeping my mind on the tasks before me. One thing that helped me tremendously was talking to God. I was able to share with Him about my restlessness and distractibility. I told Him how I felt overpowered at times by my thoughts, worries, and circumstances. How it seems like there's not enough time in the day to achieve and master all He has set before me. In His usual comforting way He said, "Brooke, call upon Me when you are weary, burdened, or have no strength, and I will help you." As I reflect today over His statement, I have always found this to be true. Whenever I call on Him and talk with Him, I feel refreshed and am reminded of His care over me and His provision for me. I'm also

reminded that I don't have to do it all alone—that God works for me and with me to accomplish anything He has asked me to undertake.

He talked with me a great deal about continuing to place my trust in Him and, as I do, to rest. I know I need rest of body, but it had never occurred to me to rest the soul or the mind. I have certainly experienced the value of physical rest during this time of development. The more I rest and the better the quality of my rest, it seems I can accomplish my building projects with precision and strength. The opposite is true when I fail to rest properly. I find that I work slowly and ineffectively. My difficulties increase, and my mind becomes cloudy and distracted.

I've started to discover that I need more than physical rest to be at peak performance; I need rest of the soul. I need spiritual rest, which can only be found in time spent with God. It's when I'm with Him in conversation or silence that I find true energy and peace. When I trust in God, or better yet rest with Him, I find I have a strength and depth of soul unmatched by anything else. It's so empowering and liberating. It reminds me of something He said to me yesterday, "Brooke, My yoke is easy, and My burden is light." It's true—I don't feel any of the difficulties of life when I commune with Him. When I feel burdened or discouraged, it's been my experience that the time spent with God has always lightened my burdens, not increased them. Oh, to know and remember all His counsel and secrets. God truly is an awesome Creator! Please know that this time of preparation is not being wasted, Daddy. I'm being well prepared for everything I'm going to need in life.

Yours, Brooke

DAY	WEEK	MONTH
75	11	3

Wednesday, August 7, 2002

Dear Daddy,

What's it like to walk the earth and take in God's wonders? This morning as I was working on some nerve connections, the neurons and synapses were dancing in a marvelous pattern that glimmered and sparked. I was captivated by the beauty!

The exhilarating experience prompted me to ask God what else He has created besides people, and He told me about the heavens and the earth. I was undone by what He described. My imagination was overwhelmed as I tried to grasp the beauty of trees or the great distance of flowing rivers. I felt intimidated as He talked about the towering mountains and the great canyons of the earth. I can't fathom the vastness of the ocean. He said, "No one has journeyed to the springs of the sea or walked in the recesses of the deep." There is water in the womb, but I can't imagine the abundance of water that encompasses the earth. Who could live long enough to take in all its grandeur and discover all its mysteries? I suppose only God. When He spoke of flowers and colors, it was a sensation overload. I wept as He spoke of the canvas of beauty that awaits my developing eyes.

God told me it would take eternity to tell me about all the splendor and majesty He has placed in the heavens. I got the feeling that the oceans of earth were but a trifle compared to the lavish works of the universe. The sun, moon, and stars sound extraordinary in their design and brilliance. I can't wait to live with you and Mommy on such a glorious planet like Earth—to bask in the sun and swim in the ocean or climb the great mountains. To lie on the cool grass and watch the radiant moon sweep across the sky as the stars flicker and dance overhead. Oh, to see what you see, Daddy! It must be glorious, penetrating, and beyond compare.

I'm so excited by what lies ahead for me. But I mustn't forget the amazing things that happen here. My nervous system is developing millions of neurons every minute. Each day I grow more integrated and functional. My heart is beating more than 150 times per minute as my body churns out miracle after miracle. Before I wrote this entry, I was looking over God's blueprints for my eyes, and I was stunned to discover that upon completion my retinas will contain around fifty billion light-sensitive points. And if that's not enough to stir you, my ears will consist of 240,000 hearing units when they're finished. God's work is so detailed and impressive. How can we keep from worshiping Him? There is none like Him—He stands alone!

Yours, Brooke

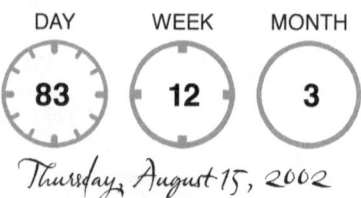

DAY	WEEK	MONTH
83	12	3

Thursday, August 15, 2002

Dear Daddy,

I'm having the time of my life. My coordination and reflexes have developed to the point where I can bounce and spring off the walls of the womb. It's so much fun to flip and twirl inside Mommy. The joy I feel radiates through my whole body as I jump and leap. It's like an internal giggle that builds and builds until I'm rolling in blissful laughter. I love to test my reflexes and see how responsive and strong I'm getting. Sometimes I float weightlessly until my legs touch the bottom of the womb, and then I spring upward as my legs impact the floor with coiled power and energy. It's great to twist and turn and move in space. The joys I'm beginning to realize as I gain greater mobility are awesome!

I can only imagine the feats I'll be capable of when I'm living outside the womb. It will be so fun to run and leap and play in the forest or at the beach. Although, I wonder if anything on earth will match the wonderful elasticity of the womb. It's so cool! I feel completely safe inside the womb and unafraid to attempt any trick my mind can imagine and my body can perform. Do you have special places where you play on earth, Daddy? I think there has to be—playing is just too fun not to continue once you're outside the womb.

Thinking about all the things God's created has made me wonder if people on earth make things, too.

Do they have the ability to create like God, or do they lack the power? Sometimes I feel like I could change what God has given me into something different or create another use for it. My mind, in an ever-increasing way, seems to constantly produce new thoughts, imaginings, or ideas. I feel in my soul that I possess a creative potential that will grow and abound more and more as I reach maturity. Maybe I'll never reach my full capacity but will continue to grow for as long as I exist. How fun—to grow and learn and create forever! Life is a trip, a great journey of perpetual discovery and joy. Being alive, being human is a great gift from God. How can we ever repay Him for His goodness to us? His choosing to create us—allowing us to enjoy this marvelous opportunity called life. I'm very grateful to Him for everything He's done for me.

Yours, Brooke

DAY	WEEK	MONTH
87	13	3

Monday, August 19, 2002

Dear Daddy,

I'm very excited today because God told me I'm about to start a major growth spurt. Over the next three weeks, I'll experience greater motor control, increased skeletal rigidity, and, in addition to improved size, the production of hair. I fancy myself quite beautiful already, but what will I look like with the elegant adornment of hair? I just know it's going to be wonderful—a thick luscious head of hair to highlight my feminine qualities and attract attention. No doubt the finished product will be worth the wait.

God also confirmed my suspicions about my creative abilities. He told me I was designed to be creative and to create. He said, "Brooke, you are made in My likeness, in My very own image." I was totally taken back by this revelation. What an honor and a privilege it is to be made in the image of God! I did find out, however, that we're not identical in many ways, especially in power, ability, and substance. Nevertheless, that I am made even a little bit like Him is incredible.

He explained that He is the only Creator that is able to create from nothing. In fact, all He needs to do to create something is speak. I've witnessed this on a few occasions, and it is most impressive. Mysterious and awesome! While not exactly like God, I'm created to be creative with what I encounter or possess. In other words, I have the ability to manipulate and use what God has already created to create new things by combination, imagination, or discovery. He created my soul and my brain and the ability to think, and I created this written diary from those given resources. In a sense, we work together to create many beautiful and helpful things. Still, God is the beginning of everything when you trace it back to its foundation. He, in effect, is the Source of all things—the Author and original Founder of life.

It's great to have a relationship with Him, to be able to consult Him and learn from His wisdom. It's so comforting to know that He is with me—that I am never alone. I like having a relationship with Him, and I know He enjoys having one with me. I think I was made for relationship, and I can't wait to experience this same kind of intimacy with you and Mommy and other people whom God has created. My soul delights in fellowship, and it seems to fit me. Know this, Daddy: My soul is eager for the day when we can converse and share in the beauties and mysteries of life.

Yours expectantly, Brooke

DAY | WEEK | MONTH
89 | 13 | 3

Wednesday, August 21, 2002

Dear Daddy,

I have begun the interesting work of myelin production. This fatty protein coats my nerves and allows for insulation and greater transmission of stimuli throughout my body. With just a small portion of the work accomplished, I am already experiencing increased responsiveness in those areas using the myelin. It's awesome how each new step in my development allows me greater control, security, and specificity. It's as if cells, chemicals, and layers build onto and into each other to allow me greater and greater freedom and capacity.

Yesterday God was examining me to test my responsiveness. It was fantastic to feel God's touch and share another tangible connection with Him. His warmth permeated my body with a welcome presence and power. I would bend and flex, grasp and kick, arch and curl, in response to His taps, tickles, and touches. When He tapped my knee, my lower leg would shoot out and kick. If He placed an object in my hand, I would grasp it and hold it tight.

The improvements in my body's capabilities and movements are huge. The things I can do after only three months of work are staggering. But the potential they hint at for the future is what really excites me. I can see, each day, just how awesome and splendid my body and mind are going to be. The things I shall be able to do will be beyond compare. I should think no other work of creation, save other people, will be able to compete with me in terms of functionality, faculty, and creativity. I and others like me are the crown jewel of God's creation!

I'm thrilled thinking of the day I'll appear outside the womb—to feel my body in all its glory and to use all of the highly specialized equipment God has given me. To experience the seamlessness of its function and to delight in the things I hear and see. Not to mention, the joy I'll experience as I bask in the companionship of family—to finally be able to fellowship with you and Mommy. What elation will be ours! Oh, I'm so looking forward to that day with you both.

Yours, Brooke

Letters to My Dad

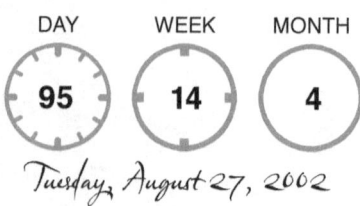

DAY — 95 WEEK — 14 MONTH — 4

Tuesday, August 27, 2002

Dear Daddy,

This morning I was jolted out of sleep by a frightful bump. When I gained consciousness enough to fully recognize what was happening, I could see the walls of the womb being pushed in on me! I was grateful for my increased mobility because it allowed me to dodge and squirm away from these round protrusions into Mommy's womb. At first it was alarming, but then I remembered God was in control, and I began to relax. Anyway, after a short couple of occurrences, it stopped. I don't know what or who was pushing on Mommy's tummy, but I'm glad it stopped. As I grow bigger, I'm becoming more aware of what goes on outside Mommy's womb. Each day, I develop greater spatial awareness and sensitivity.

Did I mention the last time I wrote that I'm starting to work on my breathing? While I'm not able to breathe like you yet, my respiratory muscles are exercising regularly. This will allow my lungs and diaphragm to have the strength and capacity necessary to receive oxygen once I'm outside Mommy's sanctuary of protection. I've been working consistently on this breathing regimen by using the fluid in the womb for over two weeks now. God said, "Brooke, if you don't prepare for the breath to come, you won't be able to receive it at the proper time." He further said, "My child, I give to all mankind life and breath and everything. Every person and all creation has its appointed time." Since I know His words are true, I've been working hard to prepare for the breath to come.

I hope I'm doing everything right. There is so much to learn and absorb and do. I constantly have to apply what I've already learned to stay the course and complete the missions laid out before me. I know it's only through collaboration with God that I will succeed in my development and growth as a person. Continuing to place my trust in Him, I will rest in the knowledge that He is capable of doing what He says. I'm so glad I'm not alone in this journey or that this process is not blind, but rather highly planned and determined. God knows what He's doing, and I, for one, am grateful!

Yours, Brooke

DAY	WEEK	MONTH
100	15	4

Sunday, September 1, 2002

Dear Daddy,

Pride goes before a fall! Two weeks after the production of hair started in earnest, I barely have any to speak of. And what I do have is thin and fine with absolutely no ability to hold or maintain its shape. Distraught, I checked the blueprints again regarding my hair, and my worst fears were confirmed. The luscious, wavy thick locks that I had imagined are sadly not destined for me! Much to my chagrin, it seems, God has ordained rather straight and thin hair for me. So much for my career as a beauty queen!

On the flip side, though, my legs are very long and shapely. I've grown to almost 6 inches in length, and my arms and legs have rounded into form nicely. I'm also starting to develop nails to complement my cute little toes. I just love to wiggle and separate my toes. I have very flexible, coordinated toes. Daddy, do I favor you or Mommy with my toes? Something tells me it's Mommy, but, regardless, I like them. I hope they never cease to provide me with amusement and balance.

I wonder what it will feel like when I first place my toes on the surface of the earth. How much will I be able to receive and process from the sensation of touch? Will it be hard or soft, warm or cold, squishy or coarse? My sense of touch is developing nicely. I can already feel and process the walls of the womb and the fluid I reside in, but I know my sensations are limited by this watery environment.

Ah, something else to look forward to when I come forth from the womb: unlimited sensations. All my sense organs unbridled and set free to interact with the world about me. To touch, see, hear, smell, and taste the things of the world that both God and man have created will be an immeasurable delight. What's it like, Daddy? I can only imagine the things you get to do. I hope you never take it for granted that you're privileged to be alive on the earth—blessed by God with the simple and awesome joys of living. In the midst of my preparation and my work, I long for the open air, for home, for Mommy, for you, for everything…

Yours, Brooke

DAY   WEEK   MONTH

105   **15**   **4**

Friday, September 6, 2002

Dear Daddy,

Since week 10, I have been working on my finger-prints, which are now almost complete. It's been fun to work on the little designs that spiral from the center of my fingers in a maze. God told me my patterns are mine alone and that no other human would have the same design. It's stunning to realize I am unique, unequaled, and entirely distinct from every other work of creation God has developed. I am one of a kind. An original work of God—set apart for His pleasure and purposes.

Knowing this, I began to think about what my purpose is and why God created me. Why does He do it? Why does He give us life? I asked Him why He created me, and He said, "Brooke, I created you to love. I created you to have relationship with Me and with others." He then added, "Brooke, all people are created with the capacity to give and receive love." He told me He loved me and that He was hoping I would choose to love Him back. He then expressed His hope that I would choose to love you and Mommy and other people whom He has created. He said, "My child, the greatest force in the universe is love! You will find no greater fulfillment in life than to love others the way I have loved you."

I think I understand what He means because He has been so good to me and made me feel so special and cared for since the first moment of my life. His love for me has been evident in everything He has done for me and provided me with. I feel treasured by Him, as if I'm a priceless heirloom—someone He values highly.

I can see how good it is to love—to treat other people the way I've been treated by God. Giving of myself in order to better their lives and bring them joy. Hoping they will return my love but not demanding them to. Hoping that, as they, too, experience love, they will love.

I told Him that I did love Him and appreciated everything He has done for me. And then I said that I loved you and Mommy, too. And He said, "I know." It feels good to love and be loved. I can't wait to express my love to you and Mommy face to face—to hear in your voice that same satisfaction that was in His. What could be better than to live and love? God has good plans for me and for all of us, Daddy. It's good to be alive and be loved.

Yours lovingly, Brooke

DAY	WEEK	MONTH
110	16	4

Wednesday, September 11, 2002

Dear Daddy,

Is something wrong with Mommy? She seems different today. There is more tension in her body, and I sense a slowness in her movements. As I grow more integrated and functional, I'm more aware of how Mommy is feeling. Her emotions seem complex and varied, but, for the most part, she comes across as steady and content.

What's it like to carry a baby inside your body? Is it uncomfortable or strange? Does it bring about anxiety and fear as well as elation and joy? Are moms ever taken by surprise, or do they know exactly what is happening and why? Is it obvious when a woman is with child, or can others tell? I know, to this point, what it feels like for me physically, emotionally, and spiritually to be inside the womb, but what does it feel like for Mommy? Is she filled with wonder? I hope it's a good experience for her. Full of expectation and joy—everything she hoped it would be.

One of the projects I'm currently working on is the construction of my uterus and the germ cells that will allow me to become pregnant when it's my turn to have a child. I don't know how or when it will happen, but I know I want to have a child of my own—someone to love and cherish and spend time with. It's exciting just to think about it. Imagining all that we might do together—how we will look, where we will live, and all the fun we will have together.

Something is happening! Mommy's tummy is fluttering with vibration. I can feel the warmth of her hands on her tummy as it heaves and pauses, heaves and pauses in little ripples. I'm worried about her, Daddy. Something isn't right! I'm going to find God and ask Him what's going on. Please take care of Mommy. Are you with her? I've got to go. God will know what to do.

DAY 114 WEEK 17 MONTH 4

Sunday, September 15, 2002

Dear Daddy,

The last three days have been very illuminating and difficult for me. God told me Mommy had been crying as she observed the anniversary of a terrible tragedy that took place a year ago on September 11. He told me that almost three thousand people, including some children, were killed by wicked men in the country that our family lives in. He said, "Brooke, your Mother was moved with compassion for the victims and their families as she reflected on the tragedy." After the initial relief I experienced knowing that Mommy was not in any danger, I was shocked and startled by what God had shared with me.

I was stunned by the revelation that people, whom God has created, would willingly take away innocent human life. Given the beauty, privilege, and joy of life, I was overwhelmed by the thought. How could anyone destroy life? How could they forget its preciousness and value? Surely they were made by the same God that made me. Didn't they receive His counsel and recall their time in the womb? Hadn't they spoken with God during their formation, just like me?

As I tried to understand these things, God told me the world I was being prepared for was not as He had originally hoped for it to be, but as a consequence of man's early rebellion, it was in a state of corruption.

He said, "I have set before people life and death, the blessing and the curse, and as a result, humans are free to choose good or evil, love or hate." He went on to say that to love genuinely, people must be free, and that liberty allows for both great goodness and terrible wickedness. He told me not to worry, however, because, while people can, and often do, choose wickedness, He is in control, and that regardless of what people choose, He has chosen to love. He said, "My child, I am good to all, all things are under My dominion, and when the time is right, I will see to it that justice is rendered."

"But how," I asked, "could anyone forget the splendor of living and the love You have shown them in the womb?" God answered, "People are slow to perceive things outside the womb. In general, I have not granted humankind the capacity to remember their time before birth." "In fact," He said, "very few people can recall, with clarity, the details of their early childhood." This information prompted me to ask Him, "God, how can anyone know You outside the womb?" "I am continually speaking to the people of earth through the things I have made," He replied. Explaining further He said, "The heavens and the earth declare My glory. My Son and the people who believe in Him declare My glory to the peoples of the earth. My Spirit and the Book I have inspired continually speak of Me. Furthermore, I have made a way for mankind's redemption and return to Me. Remember, Brooke, I bring life out of death!"

Perhaps what staggered me most was the revelation that life is limited and that I will die—that you and

Mommy will die, and that life on earth is not forever. The beautiful joy, blissful discovery, and grandeur of living will come to an end. It hurt to know that someday I will cease to live! I thought to myself, "How can this be? Why would God take away life?"

So I asked Him, and He told me, "Brooke, like water spilled on the ground, which cannot be recovered, people are appointed to die." But then He said, "I, however, do not take away life; instead, I devise the means by which a banished person may not remain estranged from Me." God went on to tell me how He provides redemption and life in heaven for all the people who believe in Him and place their faith and trust in Him. "Brooke," He said, "I am the Way, the Truth, and the Life." His last words on the subject were these: "Life and life abundant are found in Me and Me alone!"

What I understand now is that death is a part of life and that how we choose to partner with God is the determiner of our future existence with Him. If I am hearing Him correctly, it means that my body and brain, which I'm working so hard to build, are temporal, but my soul, present from the very first instant of my existence, is eternal. And that if I want to spend eternity with Him, I must continue to trust Him and know Him, believing His words. Before He departed, I asked Him if He shared this information with all preborn children. He said, "No, not all, but certainly to all who ask." And then He said something remarkable: "Brooke, I have set you apart. Before you were conceived, I chose you to bear witness to the truth of life in the womb." Then He told me, as before, to trust Him and to continue to write about my life in the womb. He said, "Brooke, you are one of My witnesses."

Daddy, I'm overcome with the purpose God has laid out for me—with the calling He has entrusted to me. This work I've been doing is more than just a diary—it's a testimony to preborn life, to God, and to the truth of human experience in the womb. Overwhelmed, I asked God to help me accomplish this task and to fill me with His strength going forward.

Daddy, do you and Mommy trust God? I hope so. It would be terrible for any one of us to miss out on spending eternity with Him. I love you, Daddy! I love you, Mommy! My longing to be with you is even more accelerated now that I know our time together on earth will be limited. I look forward to the day of my birth with great expectation—to feel the warmth of your embrace. But I don't want our embrace or fellowship to end. If you or Mommy don't already trust and believe in God, please do it today so that we will never be parted and always enjoy one another!

Yours, Brooke

DAY	WEEK	MONTH
120	18	5

Saturday, September 21, 2002

Dear Daddy,

I've never juggled so many projects at one time. Without the help of God and His literal power over time and space, I would be buried under an avalanche of responsibilities no one could accomplish. To recap: My arms and legs are elongating to their final proportions before birth; my uterus is forming rapidly along with my feminine organs; my fingers and toes are functional, distinct, and fascinating; my brain is continuing to integrate with my nervous system and gaining greater control of my body systems; my heart is growing larger and stronger with each passing day; blood is circulating freely through my entire body; and my digestive system is connected and absorbing nutrients through the intestines. I am also starting to produce small amounts of waste, which is too complicated and gross to spend any time articulating. My bones are enlarging and hardening. My lungs are creating airway branches, and many tiny air sacs are beginning to form. I'm producing brown fat to provide insulation for my important organs and body systems. God has developed a coating for my sensitive skin called vernix, which protects me from the watery environment of the womb and my growing fingernails. In addition, my entire body is now producing tiny little hairs that allow me greater temperature retention. I am quite literally a factory of cells and genes and neurons and organs and tissues. I am a sight to behold—a true work of art!

Don't worry, Daddy, I still take time to rest and play. I'm amazed at all that God is helping me accomplish with my body and mind. It blows my mind to contemplate all that has transpired in my development over the past 17 weeks. I am a miracle of engineering, construction, and capacity. I'm beginning to believe my creation is on par with that of the earth—truly breathtaking and staggering! I hope you're enjoying this account of my life and that, like me, you are filled with a sense of awe and wonder at the miraculous plans of God.

I'll try to write again soon, Daddy. It's just so hard to find the time and energy to reflect and write. Life seems better when it's not so busy, don't you think? I like it better when there is enough going on to keep you engaged and challenged, but not so much that you can barely keep your head above water (no pun intended).

Yours, Brooke

DAY	WEEK	MONTH
123	18	5

Tuesday, September, 24, 2002

Dear Daddy,

All the things I've learned so far about life and death have prompted me to ask so many questions of God. He has revealed many things to me, but I know there is much more He could tell me if He wanted to. At one point in our discussion, He said to me, "Brooke, some of the mysteries belong solely to me, the secret things."

I did, however, find out that the average life span on earth for a human being is around 70 to 80 years. I thought that was a pretty good amount of time, considering how much activity I've packed into the last four months of development, until He told me that at one time humans could live to be 900 years old.

When I asked Him why life on earth had diminished, He said, "Sin brings death." A point He reinforced by saying that from the beginning of people's choice to sin, life had been diminished and decreased. I'm having a hard time understanding the concept of sin, which He said is normal for a child in the womb because it is our greatest time of innocence. As far as I can discern, sin is disturbing to God and hurtful to people. God said, "Brooke, you will understand these things much better if you grow to maturity on earth, especially if you measure your earthly experiences against the truth I've revealed in My Book." Yet another thing I have to look forward to, and I know I'll have to wait for. Apparently, life in the womb and beyond is full of waiting.

I've gotten off track. I want to get back to what I have learned about the length of human life. What I really wanted to know is how much time we would have together as a family. If people only live on earth for about 70 years, then how much time could I expect to share with you and Mommy? I wondered how old you both were—how much life you had already lived? Then God said something I didn't expect, He said, "Earthly life can end at any moment. Brooke, no one is guaranteed a certain amount of time together." He made it clear that people need to cherish the time they're given because everyone's life is short. I asked Him, "How short?" And He said, "A person can die anytime, from the first seconds after I create their soul to the crown of old age."

I understand now I could die anytime, even here in the womb. But, ironically, I'm not afraid because I've learned I can trust God to take care of me. I've learned that those who put their trust in Him live forever in His care. This He confirmed when He said, "Brooke, I am a just God, and all people who die in the womb or during their childhood come immediately to Me and live for all eternity with Me." This knowledge brought me great comfort and solidified in my mind that God is indeed good!

Even though I know God is good and I've had a wonderful time with Him, I long to live a full life with you and Mommy. To experience the joys of earth and

live the life God intends for me there with joy and exuberance—to swim in the ocean, to walk in the forest, to gaze at the stars. How fortunate are all who get to taste the free gift of life outside the womb! Sobered by the knowledge that any one of us could die before my birth, I still believe we will be together as a family. I'm coming, Daddy, and I can't wait!

Yours lovingly, Brooke

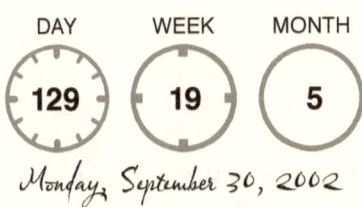

DAY 129   WEEK 19   MONTH 5

Monday, September 30, 2002

Dear Daddy,

I wonder if Mommy has let you feel me move inside of her? I know she is aware of my movements. Now when I make certain movements in the womb, I can feel her hands push back. Their warmth and presence provide me with such a tangible connection to her. I love to be touched by her, even though we are separated by the veneer of her abdomen and skin.

Sometimes when her hand is spread flat on her tummy, I place my hand against the wall of the womb under the warm spot and glory in the moment. It is as if I can hear her say, "I love you, my child, and I'm here for you. I'm waiting for you, and I love you with all my heart." If she could hear my reply, she would hear me say, "I'm here, Mommy, and I'm coming to you soon!" I love her, Daddy. She fills my heart with joy as I think of all she does for me—the things she endures for my sake. She is my mother, my friend, my hero. Without her willingness to be used by God to provide for my needs, I could not develop as I should. She is courageous and giving, and I am grateful for her care.

If you haven't felt Mommy's tummy when I move, I hope you do so soon. It is delightful fun to play hide and seek with each other through the womb. For each party to know and experience the other through the veil is a thrill and a boon to the soul. A taste of the glorious communication that awaits us upon my appearing! Can you hear me call to you? I am here, and I love you!

Yours, Brooke

DAY	WEEK	MONTH
132	19	5

Thursday, October 3, 2002

Dear Daddy,

My muscles, bones, sinews, tendons, and cartilage are all progressing nicely, and my movements have become robust and coordinated. I exercise routinely and often to improve my strength and flexibility. I love the energy and vitality exercise brings me. I can feel my body increase in power as I flex, stretch, and move about in the womb. My energy surges, and my feats increase as I build muscle and stamina.

Exercise is a great way to release tension in my body and sharpen my mental abilities. I think clearer, faster, and more precisely when I get a healthy amount of exercise and rest. It seems that each part of the body, mind, and soul are designed to work together to sharpen, shape, and benefit one another—all one unit with distinct roles and manifestations. Every part of my person is indispensable with no part being more or less important than another. I am the sum total of my soul, mind, and body, and the greater they harmonize, the better I feel and the more splendidly I function.

God has planned me out perfectly, and the further I develop, the more I recognize the intricate beauty of His design and His plans. He has made me for earth, and He has made me for eternity. He has made me for fun, and He has made me for work. He has made me weak, and He has made me strong. He has made me

dependent, and yet, He has given me my independence. He's made me to love, and yet, I'm allowed not to love or return love. God has created me to be free! He has given me life and is graciously helping me develop the tools, systems, and knowledge I need to exercise my liberty. God is a gift-giver, and what I do with His gifts is up to me. Oh, how He loves me!

I want to be like Him. I want to drink-in His counsel and learn from His wisdom. I want to model my life after His. Who better to model than God? Who better to follow than the Life-Giver? He knows how I'm formed and He knows what I need. To know Him is to know beauty, truth, life, and all things.

I'm so glad for this time of preparation, learning, development, and growth. Without its foundation, I would be ill-prepared to flower into the person God has fashioned me to be. I would lack the capacity, function, confidence, and trust to grab hold of the world He has prepared for me. Life is a priceless, precious gift, and each day I understand its value more and more.

Yours, Brooke

DAY	WEEK	MONTH
137	20	5

Tuesday, October 8, 2002

Dear Daddy,

In an environment where the miraculous happens every day, it's hard to distinguish something as truly miraculous, but I think today's events qualify. My ears are complete! I no longer have to rely on the Spirit of God to supply my hearing. I can hear with my own ears. The sounds of the watery environment of the womb are inexplicable. There are sounds I have no words for, but there are other sounds, too. Amidst the gurgles, sloshes, and slurps, I can hear the distinct beats of Mommy's heart and my own. Mine racing and fluid like a high performance machine and Mom's steady and true like a classic. It is awesome to hear! These auditory sense organs God and I have fashioned are truly remarkable.

God said, "My child, your hearing sensitivity and definition will continue to improve as you develop—you will be able to hear with greater depth and clarity the world inside and outside of your Mother's womb as you progress." Even now, I can hear the faint sounds of things beyond the womb. But their volume is drowned out by the sounds close at hand. Needless to say, I am eager for my hearing ability to improve to the point where I can separate and distinguish the sounds I'm receiving. I'm super excited to hear the sound of Mommy's voice and yours.

To hear the voice of God with my own ears was exceptional! His voice is a mixture of both incredible power and hushed softness. Depending on His tone or inflection, it is the most intimidating and comforting thing one can imagine. His voice commands respect, and yet it makes you feel safe. There are no adequate words to describe the timbre, weight, and veracity of His voice. His voice can leave you speechless, and as much as I have tried to explain it here, I know I have failed to do so.

What a delight my ears are to me! Like my heart, brain, fingers, and toes, they are a beauty to behold and experience. I shall never get over the intricate workings of God and His marvelous goodness to me. How privileged am I to be writing about my life in the womb to you. This grand adventure gets better every day. Listening for you, Daddy!

Yours, Brooke

DAY	WEEK	MONTH
142	21	5

Sunday, October 13, 2002

Dear Daddy,

I heard Mommy sing today! It was quiet, and suddenly I felt the warmth of her hands on her tummy, and then a few moments later, the sound of a song. She sang so softly and sweetly. The following are the words she sang:

"Jesus loves you this I know,
For the Bible tells me so.
Little ones to Him belong,
They are weak but He is strong.
Yes, Jesus loves you! Yes, Jesus loves you!
Yes, Jesus loves you! The Bible tells me so.

Little child of mine be strong,
God will bring you safely along.
You are born of His design,
Sent to me through space and time.
Yes, Jesus loves you! Yes, Jesus loves you!
Yes, Jesus loves you! The Bible tells me so.

I'm so glad that you are mine.
I'll gladly sing this nursery rhyme.
Bestowed on me, my child, my love,
A precious gift sent from above.

Yes, Jesus loves you! Yes, Jesus loves you!
Yes, Jesus loves you. The Bible tells me so.

You are mine and I am yours,
To have and hold forevermore…"

I don't know how to convey the melody, but it was beautiful. It was one of the best moments of my life to have Mommy sing to me with love in her heart.

I was undone by what she felt for me—to realize what I had hoped and dreamed was true. To know my Mommy loves me and that she is as excited about me as I am about her. It was bonding and joyous! The gift of my completed ears has brought me more than I could have imagined. They have brought me a wider understanding of my Mommy and a richer intimacy with her.

I'm so grateful for the gift of hearing. It has brought me even closer to my mother than I was before. How sweet to know her—to hear and experience her in a different dimension.

Yours forever, Brooke

Monday, October 14, 2002

Dear Daddy,

What's happening today? I hear many voices, but they're hard to distinguish. Even Mommy's voice seems to get lost in the various sounds and voices. I can tell there is a great flurry of activity and excitement. Amid the chatter, I hear laughter and some deeper sounding voices. Is one of them yours, Daddy? I'm still working on recognizing your voice when I hear it. Mommy's voice is the easiest to hear and recognize because it is the closest to my ears. Listening to you and Mommy talk last night helped me get an idea of your voice, but I still lost some of your words and tone. I know my hearing will become more acute as I mature, but for now I'm having trouble separating out all the sounds.

Wait a minute! I can hear something quite well at the moment. All the voices have blended into one. Everybody is singing…"Happy birthday to you, happy birthday, dear Charlie, happy birthday to you." I've lost the clarity again as the people have returned to cheers and chatter. Who's Charlie? Has he just been born? Or are you and Mommy celebrating the day he was born in the past? When I get the chance, I'll ask God about what's happening today outside the womb.

Whatever is going on, I'm enjoying all the liveliness, even if I can't quite make out every word or sound

with clarity. Hearing is such a great tool of the body and one in which I take great delight.

I'm going to stop writing and just enjoy the experience. It sure seems like you and Mommy are having fun today. I'm glad. I like the idea of the two of you having fun together.

Yours, Brooke

DAY   WEEK   MONTH

146   **21**   **5**

Thursday, October 17, 2002

Dear Daddy,

I found out from God that you and Mommy were celebrating your brother's fortieth birthday. He told me that humans like to celebrate their friends' and families' birthdays, especially certain milestone years, and that the fortieth is a big cause for celebration on earth, as it often represents the beginning of middle age. The reason I had so much trouble distinguishing the various voices and sounds was because there were so many people at the party. It's great to know I have an uncle named Charlie, who is 40 years old. And since I couldn't express myself at the party in a way anyone would understand, I would like to say in this diary: Happy Birthday, Charlie! I look forward to meeting you.

I don't know why I didn't think about it before, with all God has already shared about people, but the thought of extended family had never occurred to me. As God and I continued to talk, it dawned on me that I come from a rather large family. I have uncles and aunts, grandparents, and cousins. I even found out that you, Uncle Charlie, and Aunt Kim were all born in October. It is terribly exciting to think of all the relationships and connections I already have through family. To realize there is a whole group of people connected to me who are awaiting my arrival is magnificent.

But the greatest discovery, the highlight of our conversation, was learning about Elijah. When God told me I had an older brother, I was overjoyed—to know that I was not your only child, Daddy, to realize that our family wasn't just the three of us, but the four of us, was awesome! Ever since my creation, I've been thinking about the future with you and Mommy, and now I realize that I will get to spend time with Elijah, too. Oh, the fun we will have together! Knowing the broader gift of family that awaits me, I'm all the more eager to complete my time in the womb and live with you all.

Is there anything better than life? Each day is filled with wonder, discovery, and joy. I'm looking forward to the future, but I'm also enjoying the present. Earlier today, I was feeling my lips and placing my fingers in my mouth. The sensations were interesting and fun. I've also started to make all sorts of movements with my mouth. The muscles of my face are well-coordinated and responsive. I can make any expression that I can imagine. My favorite is the smile. When I'm filled with joy or amused by something, I can feel my cheeks lift, my mouth broaden, and my lips separate. It's a wonderful feeling to smile.

I'm also happy to report that my eyes, still sealed and developing, are nearing the completion of their essential structure. This is a very exciting time because now I can begin the next important phase in eye coordination and development: dreaming! God's blueprints call for rapid movements of the eyes, which are achieved as a consequence of dreaming. Essentially, seeing before I can really see through the spirit of the dream. The prospect of seeing even if it's only through the mind's eye is tantalizing and thrilling! I'm so excited to dream! I'm anticipating dreaming any day now. I can't wait to be with you and Mommy and Elijah, but I also can't wait to dream. I'm looking forward to being with you soon, my family, but I'm enjoying this beautiful time of preparation as well.

Yours, Brooke

DAY   WEEK   MONTH

150   **22**   **6**

Monday, October 21, 2002

Dear Daddy,

Early this morning I awoke after a beautiful dream. The richness of the colors and the vibrancy of the dream were unforgettable. It started out with radiant beams of sunshine cascading through tall grass. Light danced as a gentle breeze blew back and forth on the blades of green—warmth radiated through the experience. A nearby tree flickered and whistled against a dazzling late afternoon sky. A sky dotted with beautiful puffy white clouds and the occasional whiffs of see-through cloud vapor. Striking clouds moved across a deep blue canvas of the most perfect hue.

In the stillness, I could feel controlled breathing and the race of a heartbeat. Suddenly, I was transported to a place inside the tall grass. My eyes darted back and forth nervously as if I were in great, but delightful, danger. The tension mounted with each passing moment as I desperately tried to control my breathing and body. Something or someone was close, and the energy and expectation were intense. As the wind started to increase in the roar of its power, I heard the faint sound of a snapping twig.

Quickly, I sprang to my feet and began to bound and skip through the tall grass. An imposing figure behind me noticed my escape and started to close fast. As they approached, I laughed and squealed with delight. My speed was at its height when I crossed the valley and began my ascent up the hill. Swift but stumbling, I made my way to the crest.

Before I could catch my breath, I was suspended above the entire scene, taking in the breathtaking view of the greenest, purest rolling hills. Arrested by the bewitching beauty of the terrain, I was lost in majesty. I don't know how long I was frozen in admiration before I heard the voice of a jovial, giddy little girl. Her voice suggested a delightful happiness as she ran from her father laughing heartily and saying, "Daddy, no Daddy, no . . ." My focus was quickly pulled to the young child and her father running through the tall grass playing chase. It was enchanting to watch the two at play.

As the young girl darted behind a tree and her father pretended to lose sight of her, the dream ended, and I awoke. Dreaming is everything I thought it would be and more—to see the earth and all its beauty, to feel the breeze across my face, to melt in the warmth of the sunshine, to run, to leap, to play. It was more than I even imagined it could be! Oh, Daddy, nothing I've experienced to this point compares to dreaming. It is glorious!

God's design continues to impress me. What better way to exercise the eye than through dreaming. And what fun—to let us see the unseen and experience from a distance things we otherwise could not. I love His plan and His process. How exquisite is this journey in the womb—truly captivating and beyond compare.

Yours, Brooke

DAY	WEEK	MONTH
154	22	6

Friday, October 25, 2002

Dear Daddy,

I'm currently recovering from a frightful bout of hiccups that occurred during my routine swallowing exercises. It seems they can happen at any time and for no apparent reason. I wouldn't mind so much if they weren't so disruptive and at times painful.

I really don't like being thrown off my routine either! My calendar is chock-full of things for me to practice and exercise. Every day I practice swallowing, sucking, breathing, tasting, dexterity, and waste removal. Not to mention all the exercises I perform to strengthen and improve my muscle development, coordination, and reflexes. Add to these continuing organ and system refinement, brain and cognitive growth, heightened nervous system responsiveness, which, by the way, has allowed me to feel the force of the aforementioned hiccups more acutely, rapidly improving sense organs, and daily monitoring the process by which each part of the body is integrated into a seamless, free-flowing collaborative system of the highest order, and you can readily see the tightness of my schedule. As always, I'm a flurry of activity and growth! In fact, I currently weigh about one-and-a-half pounds and have obtained a length of approximately 8 inches. Not too shabby for a child roughly 22 weeks old!

Still though, in the middle of it all, I find time to rest, play, and dream. Rest for me is so refreshing, a welcome break from all the activity and accomplishments of the day, something I look forward to and need. Play is pure pleasure and fun; to exercise my mind, body, soul, and imagination in creative, enjoyable ways is the highlight of my day. But nothing compares to dreaming, to step into a world I could only have guessed at and enjoy the full range of emotion, intellect, and function as an older human person is a glimpse of the glory to come and a revelation of what God is creating me to be.

Every day of my life is full and purposeful, but as I glimpse the future, I long to experience those things to come. Sometimes I want to grow up quicker than I am. I often want to experience tomorrow, today! I find it's easy to get ahead of myself. But then I hear God's words, and I remember the shortness of life and His counsel to live in the moment and cherish each hour I'm given. Reflecting on His words, I refocus and appreciate all I currently have and get to experience. In the quiet of my meditation, I hear Him saying slow down, and I'm filled afresh with contentment and gratitude.

Yours, Brooke

DAY	WEEK	MONTH
159	23	6

Wednesday, October 30, 2002

Dear Daddy,

The other day I had the strangest and most inter-esting dream. When the dream started, I was walking on the beach and listening to the crash of the ocean. As the tide approached, I stopped and braced for the impact. I absolutely loved the sensation I felt as the water rushed over my feet. And then, when it ebbed away and the sand swiftly receded from under my toes, I cringed with delight. It was so delectable that I danced and giggled each new time the tide rolled in. This went on for some time until I happened on a group of people pursuing various activities on the beach.

One group of young people was playing a game with a ball and a net. It looked like great fun as they slid, dove, squatted, and jumped for the ball. They laughed and bantered in between hits and seemed to be having a lovely time. Some people were running into the water and diving into the oncoming waves. Others were swimming, resting, walking, or playing in the sand.

Eventually, I happened upon a little boy who was making mounds with the sand and digging a trench around his various piles of dirt. Walking up, I asked if I could play, and he said, "Sure, use that bucket to shape the mounds on the back side of the castle." I said, "What's a castle?" After looking at me with puzzlement, he replied, "It's the home of kings, silly, with knights and guards and gallant men." When I explained to him that I had never seen a castle, he went on to describe for me their impressive stature, wide moats, tall towers, and massive drawbridges. His favorite subject, however, was the ancient kings and their golden crowns.

I loved building the castle. The combination of wet and warm sand was a stimulation overload and a true tactile pleasure. As I worked my way around the back corner of the structure, I bumped into a stout little person who said, "Hey, watch it!" This completely startled me because no one was there! I looked amazingly at the spot of the infraction as I pulled back, and to my continued surprise all I could see was beach, waves, sand, and the little boy I'd asked to join in play. I turned to him and said, "Did you hear that?" "Hear what?" he replied. "That voice," I said. The little boy looked at me funny, and then returned to his task. I sat frozen for a moment not knowing what to do, and then I reached into thin air and touched the arm of the hidden person next to me, who immediately exclaimed, "Let go of me! I told you this spot is mine and I'm not leaving." "Surely you heard that," I rejoined. To my dismay, my playmate said, "There's nobody here but us. Maybe you're hearing a nearby voice on a different section of the beach."

Dumbfounded and in a state of shock, I pulled my arm away and sat in confused silence. Then I watched in disbelief as my little playmate came over and sat right where the stout person had been. The person neither of us could see blurted out, "Watch it, mister!" But the little boy on the sand heard nothing and simply said

to me, "Can I have that shovel if you're done with it?" Bewildered, I began to answer him, and at that moment the dream ended.

It was a lovely yet strange dream. I don't know what to make of it. Perhaps some dreams are just odd and impossible to figure out. I wanted to record it in the diary, anyway, and perhaps someday I'll understand it. Maybe the dream has no meaning, maybe it's just random. I did love my time spent at the beach, however. Daddy, does the water and sand on earth really feel like I experienced them in my dream? I hope so. I just loved it!

Yours, Brooke

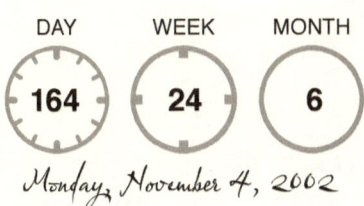

Monday, November 4, 2002

Dear Daddy,

I heard you singing the Happy Birthday song to Mommy yesterday. I'm getting much better at recognizing your voice. I like it very much that humans, especially our family, like to celebrate birthdays. A birthday truly is worthy of celebration. When I think about all that humans accomplish in the womb, they deserve to be celebrated at birth—a significant moment in the life of any person, second only to the day of their creation by God.

I loved Mommy's reaction to the gifts you gave her, especially the necklace. I didn't realize that people gave each other gifts on the day of their birth. It seems like a fun custom. I was all ears as Mommy explained the beauty of her necklace to Elijah. It sounds marvelous, with its silver chain and sparkling blue gems. You definitely made an impression, Daddy. The gift was a big hit with Mommy!

I enjoyed the rest of the party, as well. The sugar Mommy was eating gave me quite a rush of energy and giddiness. Unfortunately, after a little while it made me tired and lethargic. Later, when you and Mommy went to the movie, I was perplexed and intrigued by the different sounds I heard. The sheer loudness of the theater was both startling and engaging. I recall so many strange sounds. I didn't know what activity you and Mommy were participating in until I caught up

with God last night and He explained it to me. Humans genuinely are creative! I'm overwhelmed by all the world outside the womb holds for me—both the creations of God and the inventions of humans will be something to behold. I think the thing I enjoyed the most was the music. I loved the way it would ebb and flow—at times frantic and powerful, while at others slow and beautiful, melodic and inspiring. All in all, it was another great adventure and quite fun.

I'm so glad I found some time to talk with God after the party because our conversation cleared up a great deal and comforted me. I was feeling a little low and sad. Even though there was much to celebrate, I was feeling down that I couldn't participate more fully with you, Mommy, and Elijah. I regretted the fact that I could not give Mommy a gift on her birthday. Thankfully, God was there to brighten my mood and help me see things more clearly.

He helped me see that I already had given Mommy the greatest gift anyone can receive, the gift of myself! He said to me, "Brooke, children are a gift from Me, the fruit of the womb is a reward. People who have several children during their lives are greatly blessed. Your Mom has received no greater gift than the privilege of being your mother. She is greatly blessed because of you." I can't describe how it made me feel to know that I am a gift, a blessing, bestowed on Mommy by God. Happy Birthday, Mommy! I hope my gift sparkles far brighter than your necklace!

Your daughter, Brooke

DAY   WEEK   MONTH

167   **24**   **6**

Thursday, November 7, 2002

Dear Daddy,

Last night I had another lovely dream, but it was not without its oddities. I found myself in the middle of a giant room full of the most wonderful obstacles, inflatable slides, and trampolines. I stood amazed and intimidated by the sheer size of the equipment and the steady hum of the air machines. The diversity of color was intense and beautiful, from the silky blacks to the brightest yellows and whites. I looked around for others, but quickly discovered I was alone.

Eventually, after much observation, I worked up the courage to approach the towering slides. Dangling before me was a rope hanging innocently from an inflatable wall with recessed pockets and protruding knobs. I remember feeling the rough threads of the rope as I grabbed hold with my fingers. The bubble-like wall was taut and smooth. When I pushed or pulled on it, it resisted with buoyancy, sliding, and popping. Strangely, it reminded me a little of the womb. Proceeding at first with caution and then rapidly with exuberance, I ascended the wall and made my way to the top of the slide. My eyes grew big as I contemplated the drop. Fear crept in, and I almost abandoned the mission, but then I remembered that fear was the enemy of progress, and with great haste I propelled my body forward. The slick

slide provided a burst of speed, and I let out a squeal of delight as the wind ruffled my hair!

After several glorious rounds on the slide, it was off to the trampoline to showcase the acrobatics I had learned in the womb. The trampoline had a great springiness and elasticity. But after a couple of twists, flips, and turns, I quickly discovered that the womb is a far safer place to ply the trade of tumbling. One rather surprising and rough spill convinced me to conduct my affairs with greater restraint and caution.

Out of breath and tiring of the trampoline, I turned my attention to a collection of balls in the corner. Picking out a red one, I began to bounce it on the floor. I soon realized that the greater the force I applied, the higher it would rise. I tried my best to bounce it as high as the giant slides, but, unfortunately, I did not have the strength.

In the midst of my robust play, I was startled by a loud cheer and the stomping of several little feet. As I whirled around to look behind me, an entire group of children were descending on the play area, leaping, laughing, squealing, and bounding toward the slides, balls, trampolines and obstacle courses. I was over-whelmed by the mob at first, but eventually I began to play among the children. The play dynamic had changed, but not its joy. In fact, I found the experi-ence of company to be richer than my time alone—to interact with other boys and girls in collaborative play was quite enjoyable and offered endless opportunities for imagination and creativity.

I don't know how long we had been at play before I started to notice something odd. Various children began to disappear. Before too long, about a quarter of the children had vanished. As I stopped to appraise the situation, I became aware that none of the remaining children had noticed the disappearance of their peers. Then something amazing happened! I discovered that the missing children were not missing after all, but that they'd been misperceived by those children who remained. I could see them, but no one else could. I tried in vain to alert the other boys and girls to their veiled presence. No matter what I tried, it failed. It soon became apparent that the remaining children left in the play area couldn't hear me, either. I began to wonder if I wasn't hidden as well! Still, I had just interacted with them and I knew they had seen me. As I stood there puzzled, the dream faded, and I returned to consciousness.

Do you have strange dreams, Daddy? Is this a normal part of dreaming—the mixture of the real and the surreal? Or is there a message in my dreams? Perhaps there's something in my dreams to learn or discover. I'm sure God will know. I'll have to remember to ask Him about my dreams the next time I talk to Him. For now, I'm at a loss. Despite the mystery of my recent dreams, I love the process. It's so fun to play and live in the life of

the dream. I can't wait to have the next one, and when I do, I'll tell you all about it.

Yours, Brooke

P.S. My hearing is rapidly improving in its clarity and ability to recognize sounds at a distance. I enjoy hearing your voice when you arrive home from work, Daddy.

DAY   WEEK   MONTH

170   **25**   **6**

Saturday, November 10, 2002

Dear Daddy,

This morning I had great fun listening in on your conversation with Mommy about my future name. Of course, God has already called me by name, and I know what you'll choose, but I took particular delight in hearing your suggestions. Please, Daddy, Wilhelmina! I can only hope you're joking. Wilhelmina, along with Edith, should never enter into a proper conversation concerning appropriate names for a young girl.

Elisabeth was nice, and I rather like the name Hope, but Gertrude, yick! Grace is a beautiful name, and Hayley sounds dreamy; Mommy is right to reject Ida, it sounds sharp and cutting. Brooke, however, is a perfectly adorable name. It's smooth and cool and beautiful and endless.

I especially like what Brooke means: stream. Flowing water goes on forever. It never ends or ceases to satisfy. Streams bring you peace and remind you that you are alive, and full of power, and promise, and potential. A stream meanders and carves and leaves a mark upon the earth. It's living and active, and with each new bend it reaches toward the future, while staying firmly connected to the past. Waters carry hopes and dreams. Each stream follows a course and a plan toward an unknown destination. This, Daddy, is an excellent name!

My middle name, Anna, is also a commendable choice. It flows quite well with Brooke, and as for meaning, it's solid there, too. I appreciated your comments about the power of God's grace and mercy in your life, Daddy. Having a name that reminds me to give and receive grace and mercy is special.

I'm glad you and Mommy want to give me a strong and beautiful name. The time you'd invested was evident. I could feel your love and hopes for me as you teased one another and discussed your options. Thanks for selecting Brooke Anna. It's a beautiful name. I like it very much!

Pleased, Brooke

Tuesday, November 12, 2002

Dear Daddy,

I'm so glad you, Mommy, and Elijah enjoyed your trip to the mountains of Utah over the long weekend (although I suspect from Mommy's comments that the second fish you caught was not the three pounds you alleged). I recall a great deal of boasting and self promotion—not your most dignified or humble moment! I gathered from your comments that it was a beautiful place to visit, with a lake and a flowing stream. It also sounded like you're not too fond of the desert and our hometown of Las Vegas, Nevada.

I heard Mommy complain about sleeping in the cabin and how uncomfortable she was. It was quite clear the mattress didn't work for her. It further sounded like I'm starting to make her a little uncomfortable, and as a result it's hard for her to sleep. I hope I don't keep her up most nights, and if I do, I sincerely apologize—sorry, Mommy. I am getting larger by the day, and I can't imagine what it must feel like to have me stretching her body, sharing her food, and playing in her womb. I hope I'm not too much trouble. I do appreciate so much her provision, protection, and care over me. For what it's worth, Daddy, tell Mommy I enjoyed the delicious s'mores and milk she ate at the campfire. They provided me with a rush of giddiness and pleasure. I can't wait to taste them with my own palate.

Being able to hear you both makes me feel close to you—so much a part of the family. It's hard to wait until I can be there in my full capacity, but knowing that I will be soon makes it more bearable. Even so, sharing in the little things makes me feel included and part of the happiness that is our family. Please continue to take care of Mommy. She seems so tired lately. Case in point, I heard her snoring throughout most of the ride back to Las Vegas!

Yours, Brooke

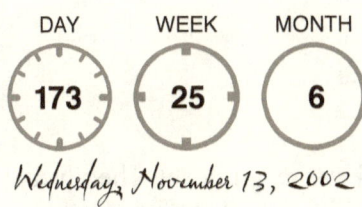

DAY   WEEK   MONTH

173   **25**   **6**

Wednesday, November 13, 2002

Dear Daddy,

Last night, I dreamed my best dream yet! I dreamed we were on a camping trip somewhere in the tall majestic mountains. You, Elijah, and I were fishing at a crystal blue high mountain lake surrounded by lush evergreens. The evening sun sparkled, shimmering on the water like an elegant dancer. Briskly, the air settled in the stillness, and a silence grew.

As I marinated in the moment, Elijah's shriek of excitement interrupted everything. "I've got one, Daddy, I've got one!" The rush of adrenaline quickly moved from Elijah to you to me, and in the distance the mighty fish leapt from the water in full view of the heavens. The fight was on! Elijah's rod bent like a rainbow from the strain and power of the great fish. His line was so tight you could make music with it. Elijah shouted, "Daddy, grab the rod—I can't bring him in." During the exchange, the tension slipped on the line, and the fish ran like a sprinter. I heard the line sing off the spool with a high-pitched, whirling sound. This was a powerful fish!

After 20 minutes of fierce running and reeling, you handed the rod back to Elijah to finish the work. Nearly 15 minutes later, the mighty fish was spent and had resigned itself to the fate of being our impending supper. The sight of this marvelous creature up front

and personal was magnificent. The silvery pink sheen of the worthy foe's scales flickered gloriously in the dusky light. As you slipped the hook from its powerful jaw, you held up the prize for us to admire. Using a tape measure from your belt, you proclaimed that the fish was over 21 inches long and (by your estimation) at least five pounds! Elijah, filled with joy, admiration, and benevolence after the epic battle, looked at you and said, "Release him back into the water, Daddy. He deserves to live to fight another day!" Agreeing, you placed him back in the lake, and we all watched in awe as he slipped away into the darkness of the water.

As we walked back to the campsite, the air was filled with happy voices, laughter, and the retelling of the great tale of Elijah and the fish. After a delightful supper and the building of a superior campfire, we roasted marshmallows and ate delicious, melty, oozing s'mores. Their taste was spectacular, better than I ever thought they could be. Each bite was a burst of warm luscious flavor, and each drink of milk was a complementary cleansing that readied my mouth for the next eager bite.

I thought nothing could top this event, but I was wrong! In the dying glow of the fire, out came the stars! Their beauty and charm was unmatched as they flickered in the heavens. Their number could not be counted, and their grandeur was overwhelming. After you doused the remaining fire, we sat in the black and beheld the wonders of God in reverent appreciation. I could have dreamed this dream forever, but, alas, I had to awake and tend to the day's tasks inside the womb. If my dreams are anything like living life outside the womb, then I'm in for the greatest adventure and the grandest life that anyone could experience. Life is a tremendous gift and a glorious pursuit. Thank you, God, for giving me life and creating me to live!

Yours, Brooke

Letters to My Dad

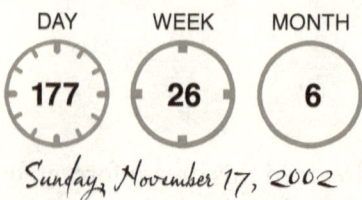

DAY	WEEK	MONTH
177	26	6

Sunday, November 17, 2002

Dear Daddy,

More great news from the womb! I have completed my eyelashes, established the neurons necessary to form the visual cortex in my brain, and begun to use my sense of smell. Unfortunately, there isn't that much to smell in the watery environment of the womb, so this powerful new ability is less impactful than the ability to hear. I suppose it will be one of those sensations I'll have to wait to experience in all its fullness. Still, it's great to know it is working and to glory in yet another piece of the puzzle that has been accomplished. I'm not quite sure of the purpose my eyelashes serve, but I like them. They are so small and cute, and, like my fingernails and toenails, which make marvelous additions to my hands and feet, my eyelashes make a handsome addition to my eyes.

I had great fun last night when you put your ear to Mommy's tummy and tried to hear my heartbeat. I could hear your delighted conversation as you made several attempts to hear my little heart. The playfulness and joy you and Mommy shared during the event was wonderful. However, nothing was better than when you exclaimed, "Shhh—I hear something! That's it! That's our baby's heartbeat!" It was a powerful moment of connection, and I loved sharing it with you—to know you are fully part of this process. It feels good to realize we're all going through this journey of new life together. What a great blessing family is! I trust we will have many more fun times like this in the future.

Yours, Brooke

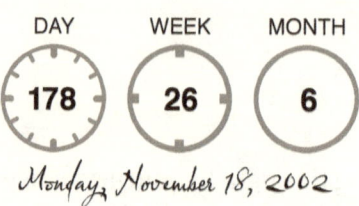

DAY	WEEK	MONTH
178	26	6

Monday, November 18, 2002

Dear Daddy,

Mommy's students can be so loud! I don't know how many students she has, but it must be in the dozens. At various points in the day, it's a barrage of conversation, laughter, and the shuffling of books and papers. So much activity and energy, I have trouble separating it all.

This morning as Mommy read out loud to the kids, there were several instances of uproarious laughter. Everyone seemed to be enjoying the story and having a good time. I even heard Mommy laugh and at times could feel her abdomen shake with little vibrating movements. It must be great fun to be part of a class—a community of peers who band together under a common purpose.

Mommy is a good teacher. She spends several hours at work each day and always helps her students who need additional instruction. I like hearing her lessons and sampling the various disciplines she teaches. I know I don't understand everything she teaches, but it's still interesting. School seems like such fun. It will be great to develop new skills and process the abundant information school holds forth. I've already learned many things in the womb, and I look forward to being able to expand my knowledge outside of it.

I think it's a great privilege to be a teacher—to lead others in their pursuit of maturity. Helping people acquire the skills and information necessary to complete various tasks, enabling them to enjoy their lives more fully. I'm proud of Mommy and her willingness to be used in a capacity that works for the betterment of people. I'm glad God chose to give me to Mommy and Mommy to me. I'm looking forward to enjoying many fun times together—times of love, laughter, and learning.

Yours, Brooke

Friday, November 22, 2002

Dear Daddy,

I've been trying, unsuccessfully, to locate God this morning. My dreams involving unseen people are back, and I need some answers. Last night's dream was not like the others—it was painful and disturbing. I'm beginning to believe that something horrible is happening! I want to know what my dreams mean and why I am having them. Since I can't get my questions answered right now, I'm going to record the dream and my feelings while they're still fresh. I hope God will come to me soon! The following is what I remember about the dream.

We were back at the lake fishing—very similar to the camping dream where Elijah caught the beautiful fish, only this time it was just the two of us. We were having a conversation, about what I can't remember, while we were sitting on some large rocks near the water's edge. The evening was still, and all seemed to be going nicely when I heard a faint voice calling. The voice was muffled and distant, almost inaudible at first. In fact, I thought it was only my imagination when I first heard it. Looking over at you, I noticed you were watching your fishing line and completely oblivious to any noise or voice. Ignoring the distant voice, I returned to my delicate fly, which was floating effortlessly on the glassy water.

Returning to our conversation, I felt confident that the voice was a phantom until I heard it a second time, a little louder than before. The voice said, "Help me." Feeling spooked, I began to scan the surrounding water, rocks, and trees for the sight of something or someone. After a few nervous moments, I turned to you and asked, "Did you hear someone calling for help?" Concerned, you replied, "No, I haven't heard anything!" At that point, we both began to search the horizon for another person or anything unusual. Several minutes passed as we looked for the source of the voice, but to our dismay we could not find the person.

Believing it was the wind I had heard, you convinced me to return to our fishing. However, you cautioned that we should remain alert, just in case we missed something. Upon my third cast, when the nervousness was wearing off, the voice came again very sharply: "Help me. Help me, please!" I dropped my rod and staggered back in apprehension. Quickly, I looked at you and discovered you were already on the move toward the sound of the voice. I shouted, "Daddy, you heard it, you heard it, didn't you?" Moving quickly you countered, "Stay put, Brooke, I'm going to have a look." Scrambling up the rocks, you reached the top and peered over the edge at the water below, but to your surprise, there was nothing there. Joining you, I noticed the water was as calm as when we had first begun our fishing.

Looking at me with amazement, you said, "Brooke, someone is in trouble. Grab my field glasses from the fishing vest and start scanning the water. I'll search the rest of these rocks and then meet you by the tackle box." Peering through the glasses, I could find nothing, but then as I was about to give up hope, I heard the voice at its loudest say, "Hurry, hurry! I'm almost out of time! Please help me!" Jerking the glasses to the sound of the voice, I spotted broken water and frantic splashing in the distance. I yelled, "Daddy, I see them! I've found them!" Rushing to my side, you blurted out, "Stay here! I'm going to get them!"

Off you ran at a furious pace, leaping over fallen logs, dodging trees, and climbing over rocks. Looking again through the glasses, I could see the splashing start to subside. I yelled out, "Hurry, Daddy! Hurry!" Strangely, I could see the agitated water and hear the person's cries for help, but I could not see the person. Like my other dreams, they were unmistakably there, but I could not see them. When you reached the other side of the lake where the splashing had been spotted, only the ripples of a frantic fight remained. Instantly, you dove into the water and swam to the last known spot of the panicked person's thrashing. After several unsuccessful attempts at rescue and recovery, you swam to shore exhausted, wet, and confused.

As I ran to meet you in a state of alarm, I saw defeat and bewilderment on your face. When I reached you, the cold had set in, and falling to your knees, you gasped for breath. Collapsing together by the shore, we stared in exhausted silence at the placid water that now concealed a person we could neither find nor help. Sorrowfully, you looked at me and expressed in resignation, "They're gone—there is nothing we can do for them now." Shocked and overcome, I felt myself leave my body. Suspended above the lake, I saw the two of us huddled together as the dream faded and slipped away.

I am very disturbed by this latest dream! It's frustrating that I haven't been able to communicate with God about it yet, but I know there is a purpose in it. These dreams with unseen people in them are not a random happening. They are intentional, and they must have a point or a message. It's just that I'm at a loss to see it. Only God can unlock these mysteries in my dreams, but until He does, it's important to write them down. As unnerving as it's been to record this latest dream, I find it's helped release some of my tension. I don't want to have any more dreams like this one, Daddy. I'll let you know when I figure out what's going on.

Yours, Brooke

P.S. This is the first dream I've had where someone besides me could hear the unseen person. You couldn't hear them at first, but then you could. What does it mean that we could both hear them?

DAY	WEEK	MONTH
187	27	7

Wednesday, November 27, 2002

Dear Daddy,

This is my third attempt to write this entry because my tears have smeared the previous two efforts beyond readability! God has shown me the mystery of my dreams, and I have been broken by His revelation. I now understand, with profound sadness, that my nation and many others around the world are intentionally killing children in the womb. All the unseen people in my dreams were preborn children. Preborn children who were not allowed to live beyond the womb! How brutal is the human race! What depravity exists in people that they would even murder their own children! I can't bear the thought of it. I am stunned, saddened, and terrified by the revelation of what people are capable of.

In the midst of our dialogue, God said, "Brooke, I've set you apart to testify to life and truth. I've given you the ability to write and speak, even from the beginning, and I want you to witness to the world about what you have seen, heard, and experienced inside the womb. Show them the beauty and grandeur of life!"

I understand now the importance of writing this diary, Daddy. I'm a witness to human life and its beginning. I hope my testimony changes things—that it's enough to rouse people from their slumber and encourage them to pursue what is right. I sincerely believe my purpose is to turn people's hearts back to their children.

I asked God why we couldn't save the drowning person at the lake, and He said, "My child, many beautiful people have already been lost to the earth, but many more will be lost if people fail to act." He went on to say that the last dream I had at the lake was designed to help me see the urgency of the matter, and that time was of the essence. He also wanted me to know that rescue involves hearing, seeing, and deliberate action. Nothing changes for the better if we fail to listen, look, and engage.

I then asked Him, "Why could I hear the unseen children in my dreams, while the people around me could not?"

He replied, "Brooke, I've given you ears to hear. Many people on earth are living with stopped-up ears. The cares of the world, the pursuit of pleasure, and an abundance of false teachings have plugged their ears and dulled their hearing."

"Is that the reason my Daddy was slow to hear?" I asked.

"Yes, but in time, like in the dream, he, too, will hear."

I asked, "God, what can I do to show a blind and deaf people the truth about life?"

Firmly He responded, "Brooke, be a witness to life!"

After letting His words sink in, He said, "Come, follow Me, I want to show you something." Immediately, I was caught up out of the womb, following this most

magnificent God swiftly through a prism of light. Suddenly, we slowed down as we entered a thick bank of clouds. As I walked through the mist, I could hear deep rumbling and sharp crackling. Nearing the edge of the mist, I noticed God had departed. Hearing the sound of singing in the distance, I pressed forward. So beautiful was the song and its melody that I was filled with intrigue and cautious anticipation. When my eyes finally broke the mist, I was immediately overwhelmed by what I saw. Falling prostrate to the ground, I covered my face and lay motionless.

A strange creature came near and said, "Open your eyes and see! Do not be afraid! You were invited here by the Ancient of Days!" Cautiously peering through my hands, I saw wonders and colors I cannot describe. I gazed upon the creatures, men, crowns, thrones, and crystal with amazement, but my eyes eventually became fixed on a great throne in the distance. As though looking through field glasses, the throne enlarged before me, and I beheld a man kneeling to the right of the throne. Dressed in the purest white, He was so powerful that I immediately looked away. Compelled, however, by the love and grace that emanated from His person, I returned my gaze upon Him.

He was speaking and groaning in a language I did not understand, but the beauty and power of His tongue were completely arresting. I could not take my eyes off Him. He was and is the most compelling being I've ever seen. After being lost in His meditations for some time, He began to weep!

Immediately, I fell to my knees and began to sob like I'd only imagined could be done. Breathless and overcome, I looked up and saw His own tears stain His garments and pool on the ground below Him. From His reservoir of tears a little stream began to flow from the throne to the earth! Then in the most lamentable sound one can utter, he said, "My children. My children!"

Undone by His compassion, I backed away and started to leave. Rising, He said, "My child, where are you going?"

Without looking up, I said, "I don't know, Your Majesty."

"Come unto Me," He said, "I have much to show you." As we walked and talked together, I felt secure, loved, and free! Much of what He shared with me I'm not at liberty to convey, but He did tell me what He wanted me to communicate to the people of the earth.

He said, "Brooke, I've commissioned you to write your diary. Continue to testify to the people of earth about life. Encourage My people to pray earnestly for the preborn children and their parents. Tell them I'm forgiving, patient, and merciful. Write to them that I am longing to forgive their sins if they will bring them to Me. Implore My people to pursue justice and rescue those children who are being led away to death!"

Before our conversation ended, I said to Him, "Great King, you seem so familiar to me, do I know you?"

"I AM like my Father. My Father and I are one," He

replied. With that He vanished in the blink of an eye, and I found myself back in the comfortable confines of Mommy's womb.

I'm glad to know that you have ears to hear, Daddy. I pray the Spirit will speak to you in the months and years to come. There is so much more to God than I know. He is beyond searching out. Each new revelation of God is deeper than the last. He is more than I can comprehend!

Overwhelmed, Brooke

Sunday, December 1, 2002

Dear Daddy,

As I enter my 28th week of life, my body is integrating fabulously, working collectively and collaboratively to perform and regulate its various functions and duties. My central nervous system is controlling my body temperature, rhythmic breathing, and all processes within my digestive tract. My bone marrow is now the main source of blood formation, taking over much of the blood duties from my spleen. My lungs have been exercised and developed to the point where I could properly exchange oxygen and carbon dioxide using the air outside the womb. I continue to grow larger, longer, and fuller, with my current weight being around 2 pounds. My skin is becoming smoother and less wrinkled. I have produced a great deal more head and body hair as I continue to develop insulating fat stores under my skin. I've also improved my brain function by establishing many critical connections. My brain growth and maturity have steadily increased my ability to retain memory and learn. My hearing is sharp and accurate, and my coordination, flexibility, and strength are ever-improving as my muscles, joints, tendons, ligaments, and bone work seamlessly to do my bidding. I'm feeling very good in mind and body and am beginning to sense the time of my completion is drawing near.

In addition, my eyes have opened and have sufficiently developed sensitivity to light. Sadly, the womb

is a dark environment, and I still need to work my eyes into shape so that I can perceive color and develop focus. For now my perception is limited to a darkened blur—not what I had been hoping for but, nonetheless, a steady improvement as I grow and develop. Admittedly, I'm primarily in the dark concerning my eyesight, but I have seen much through the illumination of God. Spiritually, I'm no longer in the dark! What I have seen in my dreams, understood with my spirit, and have had clarified by God is of great concern to me, and something must be done!

Lately, I've committed a great deal of thought as to just what I can do to witness to life. How can I shed light on preborn children in the womb and remove the veil of darkness that clouds people's hearts on earth? Nothing I've yet conceived seems workable, so I'll just have to continue to wrestle with my ideas and approaches. One annoyance, to be sure, is the amount of time I've started sleeping. It seems in these final stages of development I require more and more rest. I wouldn't mind it so much if there wasn't such urgency in my heart for the task at hand. I sense that time is short, and I long to make the most of my calling and opportunity. I'll just have to stay the course until I can devise a plan. More waiting. I'm getting tired of waiting!

Yours, Brooke

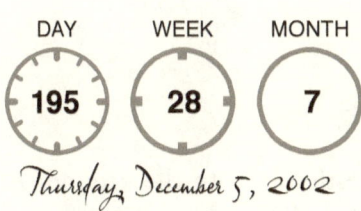

Thursday, December 5, 2002

Dear Daddy,

This morning's dream was vivid and powerful! It started out with a man threatening a woman. I could feel her fear as she cowered from his presence. Standing over her, I heard him say, "We're going to take care of this thing! You're going to get rid of it today, or, so help me, I'll make you sorry!" As his fists clenched, she melted and rose to follow him.

Before I could grasp what was happening, the scene changed, and I saw a different woman standing alone under some splashing water. She stared despondently into the distance with a look of horror and pity etched upon her face. Her despair was obvious as she slowly slid down the wall onto the floor. Sitting there in the midst of the water, she began to weep and then sob. I wanted desperately to do something for her—to comfort her—anything! Frustrated and unable to help, I cried out to God on her behalf to come quickly to help her. Returning my gaze upon her, I felt the warmth of His love coming, and then the scene washed out before my eyes.

When my vision returned, I beheld a man yelling at a young woman as she entered an isolated sterile building. As he ran toward her, he shouted, "Don't do this to our baby! Stop! There's a better way!" Just as he cried out her name, two men in uniform apprehended

him and wrestled him to the ground. After the brief struggle ended, I saw him lying face down on the ground, breathless and weeping, broken and unable to control his grief. All this was more than I could bear, and as I turned away, all became glass and standing before me was a little boy.

He was so innocent, kind, and beautiful. He was special, and I immediately felt moved by his presence. I knew instantly that he was a person of great depth and character. I could feel his love as he spoke to me. He said, "Brooke, may I show you something?"

Startled, I asked, "How do you know my name?"

He replied, "God told me you were one of His messengers and that your name was Brooke."

"How do you know God?" I asked.

"I have known God from the moment I existed and have remained with Him ever since."

It dawned on me at that moment that he was a preborn child who had never left the womb. Overwhelmed, I said to him, "Yes, I would be honored to see what you would show me." Turning, he opened up a tunnel, and we were off.

Arriving at a modest house on earth, we entered, and there before us was a beautiful young girl and her mother conversing. "It's over, my child. Stop moping, and start living again! You said yourself that awful boy you were dating forced himself on you. I never did like him, that vile creature!"

"Mom, what we did was wrong; what I did was wrong!"

"Nonsense, I will hear nothing of the sort! It's perfectly legal, and, besides, they're not human beings yet, anyway. We did this for you, sweetheart, for your future, and your life going forward. You'll see in time it was for the best for everyone."

I then watched as the young woman excused herself from the conversation and slipped upstairs. Entering the bathroom, she turned on the water and prepared a bath. As the steam from the water rose, she reached in her bag and pulled out a small bottle.

Turning to the boy, I asked, "What is she doing?"

Sorrowfully, he replied, "She's trying to take her own life."

"Why?" I asked.

"She's lost, she's filled with guilt and shame," he said.

"What has she done?"

Mournfully, he said, "She allowed me to be killed in her womb."

"She's your mother!"

"Yes," he said.

"Why did you show this to me?" I asked, puzzled about what it had to do with me.

His response was powerful. He said, "I'm hoping you can help her with your message. I love her, and

I want her to be here with me. Please tell my parents and all those who've made a similar choice about God's love and forgiveness. Tell them that their children are with God and that they long to be reunited with them. I've met many preborn children here, and they are all concerned about their parents who live on the earth."

Just as I was about to respond, I heard the door to the bathroom fly open and her mother scream, "Call 911! Oh, my baby! Oh, my god, please help!"

Before I could take another glance, we were speeding back through the tunnel to the glassy place. When we arrived, the handsome young boy looked at me and said, "Brooke, I hope people heed the words of your message. It's so important! May the words of your testimony rescue many children, help many parents, and save many souls! If your words reach my mother and father, tell them I love them and I forgive them."

As he finished his words, I awoke and wrote this account. Daddy, this tragedy is far broader than I realized, as it damages so many people. The entire family unit, and by extension the whole human race, is being devastated by this terrible practice. I hope I discover a plan to help soon; so many people are depending on it.

I hope I can help you and others discover the voice of the preborn. I wish that all people had ears to hear!

Yours, Brooke

DAY   WEEK   MONTH

199   **29**   **7**

Monday, December 9, 2002

Dear Daddy,

I've developed a plan to reveal the wonder of me before the appointed time in hopes that you will wake up to the beauty and complexity of life in the womb as you gaze at me. While there are some risks, I feel I have developed enough to survive outside the womb and will be able to continue to develop those additional improvements I need after my birth.

The things left for me to accomplish seem easy enough to finish. Besides, much of what is left for me to do I have already begun. I simply need to put on weight, finish strengthening my lungs, advance in cognitive capabilities, exercise my eyes, and add to my insulating fat stores. All those processes, I believe, I can complete outside the womb with the right care from you and Mommy. I know the womb is the safest place for me to finish developing, but I'm also aware of just how dangerous the womb can be for my peers, and this reality compels me to risk myself for their good, especially those children in eminent danger. They must desire to live life on earth every bit as much as I do!

Yesterday, as I was pouring over my developmental blueprints and checking on those things that need to be completed, I discovered the key hormone that triggers labor. When the hormone corticotrophin is produced in the placenta to the optimal level, it initiates

a process by which other key hormones are released that boost my estrogen levels, which in turn drives the onset of labor. Thus, I have decided to begin immediate increased production of the hormone corticotrophin and to prepare myself for an early birth. I'm not sure how long the process will take to complete, but I should think I will be able to arrive soon.

I believe this is my best way to speak for the preborn children and awaken your God-given ears to hear, Daddy. While admitting this is a little risky, I can't stave off my excitement to be born. No more waiting! Shortly, I will be with you and Mommy! My energy and enthusiasm to be out of the womb and tangibly on the earth is a glorious enticement. I'm coming, Daddy. Your daughter is coming quickly!

Expectantly, Brooke

DAY	WEEK	MONTH
202	29	7

Thursday, December 12, 2002

Dear Daddy,

I spoke with God this morning about my plans to initiate labor as soon as possible. My plan to leave the womb early did not surprise Him. But He did want to discuss my plan to make sure I knew what awaited me and the risks I would be taking by pursuing this course of action.

He asked me, "Brooke, are you sure you want to go?"

"Yes!" I responded.

"Very well then, I will send you," He said. "My child, there are some important things you need to know. First off, you will need medical assistance outside the womb in order to finish your development. Your lungs, immune system, and size are immature, and these realities will make your initial time after birth more precarious and difficult."

This information prompted me to ask Him, "Is the medical treatment in my nation sufficient to help me?"

"Yes, for the most part," He responded. "The nation you will be born into has great wealth, along with great technical and medical advancement. Many babies that are born younger than you do well and live long, healthy lives after their initial care."

He went on to say that the medical risks would not be the only obstacle to my premature birth. He said

the fallen state of the earth would also pose a risk to me. "Brooke," He said, "every person and creature on earth is subject to potential harm arising from disease, infection, nature, the willful or accidental actions of other people and animals, and limited understanding and knowledge." He told me my premature state would increase my vulnerability to these things. "Brooke," He said, "the way I ordered the universe after man's initial decision to sin allows all people to experience these things, and often I don't interfere with their operation upon humankind."

"Are these things you have described large causes of death upon the earth?" I asked.

"Yes, but sadly, people and animals can also willfully choose to take the life of other people, as you have already seen in your dreams."

God then went on to reveal to me something I would have never guessed. He said, "As unfortunate and as tragic as these causes of death are, they are still not the biggest source of death on the earth. Tragically, one of My highest created beings, named Satan, rebelled against Me and was cast out from My presence. It is he who is the greatest force of death on the earth. He incites principalities, powers, demons, humankind, and the elemental forces of the created order to elicit death! Brooke, be wary of Satan and those who do his bidding—he is a murderer and the father of lies, and when he lies, he is acting out of his own character and speaking his native language. My child, you must be constantly on guard against him, as he is very crafty and deceptive!"

"God, how will I know him?" I asked.

"You will know him because he does not speak the truth! Cling to the truth I have taught you and the words you hear from My Book, the Bible, and you will not fall victim to his deceptive schemes. Don't forget, you can also call to Me for help, and I will come quickly to assist you!"

The final revelation God shared with me is that I will not be able to communicate with you, Mommy, or anyone else the way I have been with Him in the womb. He told me that the power of His Spirit has made this advanced form of communication possible during my development. Once I arrive outside the womb, I will be subject to the slow developmental processes that all newborns and toddlers go through. This revelation concerned me most of all, but God reassured me that He would allow me to continue my diary through the Spirit and that He would never leave me nor forsake me. We both agreed that the living revelation of me in my developing state would still be powerful enough to awaken you, even without a word of speech spoken between us.

Daddy, I have great faith that you will see me and understand the value of all preborn children. I believe this revelation of me will wake you from your slumber and arouse you to action on behalf of the most vulnerable, needy people in our society. If God is willing,

when I reach a level of developmental competence, I will join you in the mission field for life. Together, with God, may we do great damage to the stronghold of premature death in the womb! I don't know what's to come or how well I will show forth during my birth and beyond, but I'm going to take a leap of faith and trust that God has me well in hand and that my life will make a difference.

Yours, Brooke

P.S. I now have amassed enough corticotrophin to sufficiently begin the labor process. Look for me any day now, Daddy. I'm so looking forward to being with you, Mommy, and Elijah. Nothing will be better or more exciting than my birth—I feel a celebration coming on!

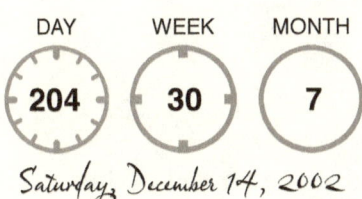

DAY   WEEK   MONTH

204   30   7

Saturday, December 14, 2002

Dear Daddy,

I feel a little better than I did yesterday, but I'm still fuzzy, exhausted, and trying hard to breathe. Yesterday was a day of alarm and triumph! Mommy's labor came on like a sudden flood in the late morning hours while she was teaching at school. I could sense her panic as she asked a coworker to cover her class and another to accompany her to the hospital. Her breathing spoke of concern and worried bewilderment as they traveled to the place of my birth. Upon arrival at the hospital, the contractions began to mount, and I could feel her strain against the inevitability of my coming. In the distance I could hear the doctors and nurses making decisions and scrambling for equipment. At last, when they determined that my appearing could not be halted, they elected to call you, Daddy, and tell you the unexpected news! Mommy held on and resisted with all her strength until your arrival and then gave in to the final stages of delivery.

Coming through the birth canal was not a pleasant experience! The squeezing and the general force of the whole journey were exhausting and stressful. Transitioning from the warmth and safety of the womb to the cold outside air was a shock to my system and a jolt to my senses. I still feel fuzzy and a little off.

I'm so glad you arrived in time to assist Mommy. She relaxed when you held her hand and prayed for us both during the delivery. I know your prayers helped us. I could tell by your tone that you, too, were anxious and overwhelmed by all that was taking place.

I wasn't prepared for the large crowd of doctors and nurses who rushed me out of the hospital room as soon as I was born. Before they whisked me away, I caught my first glimpse of you and Mommy through my blurred vision. Short as it was, it was the high point in my delivery. Still, it came at a cost; the lights burned. I'm so grateful to God for my eyelids, they helped greatly to block out the stinging brightness. My relief was short-lived, however, as the doctors pricked and prodded, attached cold patches to my skin, and shoved an abrasive tube down my throat. The pain was intense, and I gagged and started from the foreign object. I had experienced a tiny bit of pain in the womb, but this was at an altogether different level! At first, it was so hard to breathe. I gasped for breath until the oxygen and tube began to do their work. The doctors' whirlwind of activity continued until they were satisfied with their tests and efforts, and I was wrapped tightly in warm blankets, placed in a clear bubble, and transported back to you and Mommy. It was an awful experience, Daddy, much worse than I imagined it could be. I truly did not expect this much pain and difficulty, especially with my breathing.

I was greatly relieved to find myself back in your presence and hear the sound of your familiar voices.

Your lighthearted tones had returned, and it did my heart good to hear you joke with the attending doctors and nurses. I wish I could have seen the looks upon your faces more clearly. Everything was cloudy. Nevertheless, I was relieved to be close to you again. It was a great comfort compared to the strange voices and intrusive handling of the doctors.

I overheard one doctor tell you that I was good-sized for a baby girl around 29 weeks gestation—2 pounds, 13 ounces and 16 inches in length. He seemed pleased with my condition and reported that the prognosis going forward looked good. However, I was devastated to hear that the current hospital did not have the facilities required to meet the needs of a preterm baby such as myself and that I needed to be moved to a level-three neonatal intensive care unit. It disturbed me that we were to be separated again, but the remaining moments spent alone with you and Mommy softened the blow as you both declared your love for me and said a brief prayer with me before I departed for Sunrise Children's Hospital. I was further encouraged by your reassuring words that you would come soon to Sunrise to sit with me.

The ride to Sunrise was long and bumpy, and I ached each time we hit a rough spot in the road. Travel in a car is a much different experience outside the womb than inside. I must say, I prefer the latter.

When I reached the nursery, I was amazed by the beeps and flashes coming from the medical equipment. The lights were considerably softer than the ones at the

previous hospital, and it afforded me a little peek at my surroundings, but all I could see was a dim, fuzzy blur.

Upon arrival, the nurse in charge of me said, "Brooke, you'll be safe here with all your new friends. We have over 25 other preemies in the nursery with you and a great staff of doctors and nurses." She had a kind voice, and I liked her instantly. Still, it was hard to be in such a strange environment. In pain and overwhelmed, I slipped into a necessary sleep until you arrived.

Aroused by your familiar voice, I was delighted you had come. Chilled and struggling to breathe, I was very grateful for the heat lamp over my body. Thankfully, the nurse increased its output during your visit. The warmth bathed over my skin and reminded me of the warmth of God in the womb—the kind that refreshes your skin and makes you tingle with exuberant joy.

I was refreshed even more by the reading of the Bible you purchased for me on your way to Sunrise. My favorite readings were the Psalm you picked for me and the inscription you read to me from your own hand. They meant the world to me! I want to record them now in this diary so I will never forget them. First the Psalm:

Psalm 121

"I will lift up my eyes to the mountains;
From where shall my help come?
My help comes from the Lord,
Who made heaven and earth.

He will not allow your foot to slip;
He who keeps you will not slumber.
Behold, He who keeps Israel
Will neither slumber nor sleep.
The Lord is your keeper;
The Lord is your shade on your right hand.
The sun will not smite you by day,
Nor the moon by night.
The Lord will protect you from all evil;
He will keep your soul.
The Lord will guard your going out
And your coming in
From this time forth and forever."

The words of this Psalm were a great comfort to me as I lay there tired and weak.

And then you read your precious words to me:

To my daughter, Brooke,
I love you! Jesus loves you even more than me, and He doesn't make mistakes. I know He wanted you to be born today and that He will take care of you. I know this because He has taken such good care of your Mom and me. Brooke, you are very special, and I pray you will grow up to trust and love Jesus with your whole heart. Jesus is risen. He is risen indeed! Put your trust in Him. He is the Way, the Truth, and the Life.
Love, Dad.

I gathered from the other things you read and said that Jesus is God's Son. Most likely, He was the Man I met at the right hand of the throne. I can tell you from my brief encounter with Him that what you wrote is true. His love is beyond measure and without limit! Thank you, Daddy, for your kind words. I will treasure them always.

The retelling of my birth through God's gracious avenue of the Spirit has exhausted me. I must stop my writing and gather my strength. When I am able, I will write again. Tell Mommy I love her, and thanks again for being there, Dad.

Yours, Brooke

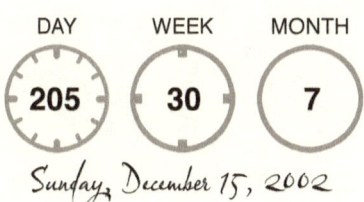

Sunday, December 15, 2002

Dear Daddy,

This morning is especially hard! I woke up alone in the NICU and could feel all the pains in my body and the fuzziness in my brain. For the first time in my life I'm feeling distant from God and angry at Him. Why am I in so much pain, and why can't I feel His presence? Why is He not here to comfort me in my distress? I know He tried to prepare me for the consequences of my decision, but somehow the reality is much harder and more bitter than I anticipated. I feel so helpless and alone.

It really is a struggle, at times, to breathe, even with the aid of the oxygen tube and other equipment. The fear of what will happen if I stop breathing and the pain in my body can overwhelm my mind at times. It's definitely harder here to trust God and walk in faith. Still, I know He watches over me. I really wish you would come and read the Bible to me again, Daddy. The words of God are a great comfort to me in my time of need, but they are useless to me unless I can hear them!

The nurse is starting to move me around and tend to my needs, so I've got to go. Come quickly to me, Daddy.

Alone, Brooke

I'm feeling so much better now that you've come back, Daddy. What a great surprise that you brought Mommy along with you! You can't know how much your visit has brightened my spirit. This morning was such a desperate time, but now with your voices close and the tenderness of your touch to comfort me, I'm relaxing. The Scriptures you've read have emboldened me to fight on and conquer these pains and obstacles that my early birth has brought upon me.

It also was a great encouragement to hear the doctor explain to you that I have a 95 percent chance of survival and more than a 70 percent chance of having no physical or mental abnormalities later in life. When the doctor was explaining to you my condition, he cleared up for me why my breathing has been so laborious. Mainly because I'm doing the majority of it! I heard him comment that I was receiving oxygen from the tube in my nose through a ventilator. He also said the oxygen was only kicking in about 10 to 20 percent of the time and that the rest of the time I was breathing on my own. I was encouraged by the fact that he said normally people breathe air with 21-percent oxygen and that my air was only slightly higher at 26 percent. Still, as encouraging as these numbers are, it's hard to breathe, and the stress and anxiety I feel are very troubling. I also learned that I'm getting food and medicine through the device inserted in my belly, which could explain why I feel tired and fuzzy most of the time. In spite of all the pains and difficulties resulting from my early birth, I am encouraged that the doctor sounded pleased with my progress and was optimistic about my continued improvement.

Unfortunately, it also sounded like I might be facing a rather long stay in the NICU over the next couple of months. This news was disappointing, but easier to take because you and Mommy were with me. I took great solace in the passage you read from Isaiah, Daddy. The one that says, "Thus says the Lord, your Creator, O Jacob, and He who formed you, O Israel, Do not fear, for I have redeemed you; I have called you by name; you are Mine! When you pass through the waters, I will be with you; and through the rivers, they will not overflow you. When you walk through the fire, you will not be scorched, nor will the flame burn you. For I am the Lord your God, The Holy One of Israel, your Savior . . ."

I must rest now. Thanks for coming, Mommy. Thanks for coming, Daddy.

Feeling better, Brooke

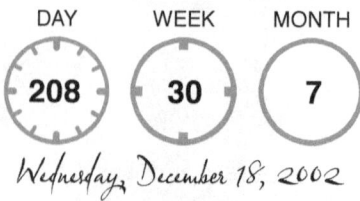

DAY	WEEK	MONTH
208	30	7

Wednesday, December 18, 2002

Dear Daddy,

Your and Mommy's frequent visits over the last several days have kept me going. My current situation is difficult as I lie in the dark feeling fuzzy, sporadically struggling to breathe. God's presence in the womb provided so much light, but here in the NICU, with my eyes covered and the lights dimmed, there is little illumination. Ever since they turned on the photo-therapy lamp for my jaundice, I've been encased in darkness with only a diminished glow around the edges of my protective eye gear to provide a hint of light. I feel I've regressed in this place. It's as if I left the realm of leaping and looking forward to enter a place of fog and shadow. Coming early has taken its toll, but if my plan succeeds, I doubt I will regret my decision.

Each day, amid the ups and downs of my physical limitations, it seems as if I'm getting stronger. At the very least, I'm getting used to the new elements of the world outside the womb and the medical devices used to provide me with aid and assistance. I'm not comfortable, but I feel more acclimated to my current conditions. Physically it is getting a little easier to manage my circumstances, but mentally the battle rages. I miss so much the ability to move about in the womb without restriction. Here it's so hard to move and breathe that I feel a great helplessness. I also miss dreaming. I have yet to dream since being born, so even this avenue of escape has not been given to me. In the womb everything was so comfortable and easy, but out here it's a battle. I don't like being dependent on the work of others and their invented machines!

In spite of my helplessness and impatience, I'm overwhelmed by the excellent doctors and nurses who take care of me. They are gifted and talented people who work long hours and take great care to make sure I am protected, covered, clean, warm, oxygenated, and provided for. I like it very much when they talk to me like you and Mommy and tell me that I'm a fighter or that I'm beautiful. I also enjoy their touch, but it can, at times, aggravate me and cause me pain. Even so, more than not, I find their interventions helpful and pleasing. Yesterday, during a procedure to draw some of my blood, I overheard the nurse praying for me, which lifted my spirits enormously. This is a great group of people, Daddy. I'm grateful for all their efforts and concern over me.

Preferring the adventure, security, and comfort of the womb, I'll admit those things exist here also, albeit to a lesser degree. Each day I learn and grow, even in the midst of suffering. Even if it's a little rougher, my adventure of life continues. Looking forward to your next visit!

Yours, Brooke

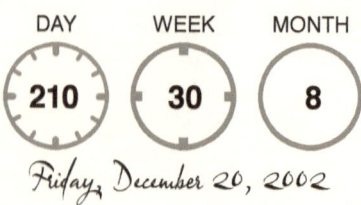

DAY	WEEK	MONTH
210	30	8

Friday, December 20, 2002

Dear Daddy,

I'm dreaming again! This time I was floating in a little boat on a greenish-blue body of water in the middle of an arid region devoid of trees and greenery. The landscape was harsh and weather-beaten, and the sun was hot and unforgiving. As the midday sun intensified and my thirst reached a fever pitch, I saw in the distance a figure like a mist coming on the water toward me. As I pressed forward to make out the person through the glare of the water, I noticed the stride of the Man at the right hand of the throne.

He was dressed in humble yet glorious clothes. I was surprised to see Him walking on the surface of the water instead of floating above it. The water splashed around His feet and licked upon the sides of His heels. Looking at His feet, I couldn't help noticing the wounds upon them. I wondered what had happened to this most perfect Being that He should be scarred so. But before I could ponder the matter, He was upon me. Startled, I looked up and said, "I'm so thirsty, Lord, give me something to drink!"

"Drink Me," He said, "and you'll never thirst again!"

I then asked, "Great King, why have You placed me in such a dry and weary land?"

His response was jolting. He said, "Such is the experience of all who seek to follow Me. It's not easy to change things, sacrifice is always required. One must be willing to die if others are to live!"

At this I cried out, "Give me strength and quench my thirst, oh King!"

Reaching down, He touched my lips, and my whole body hydrated to the point of overflow. Instantly, the entire landscape changed, and I found myself floating in the middle of a beautiful, pristine lake. The water was crystal blue with the clearest transparence. It seemed as if nothing in the water was hidden but all laid bare and made plain. I could see the bottom and the fish and the rocks and the plants with perfect clarity. The vegetation surrounding the lake was full and deep with a multiplicity of colors from the richest reds to the brightest yellows to every shade of green imaginable. The sky above shown forth a magnificent powder blue that took my breath away.

Seated in the boat with me, the King said, "Brooke, if you need Me, all you have to do is call My name, and I'll come to you and rescue you."

"Sir," I said, "what is Your name?"

He replied, "My name is Jesus." With these last words He was off, and I was back at the barren and sparse lake. Before I awoke from this dream, however, I had the distinct feeling of satisfaction, even in the dry and desolate place. God had not left me alone! He was still with me after all; I just needed to know how to find Him.

I feel so refreshed after my dream, Daddy. Mentally a cloud has been lifted from me, and I believe I can

survive this trial and accomplish my mission. Even with the doctor's news today about the intraventricular hemorrhage in my brain, I know with God's help I shall overcome. When the doctor was explaining to you my condition this morning, I finally understood why my head has felt so fuzzy. I overheard him say I had suffered a grade 2 intraventricular hemorrhage, which he said was a fancy way of saying that the ventricles in my brain had bled from a lack of oxygen during the force of the delivery, or perhaps as a result of complications after my birth due to my struggle to breathe. While concerning, it didn't sound like an unusual consequence of premature birth or like something that, over time, my body wouldn't repair and recover from. Despite his concerns regarding apnea, I was glad to hear that the doctor felt optimistic that I would continue to improve and progress toward a healthy release from the hospital.

Daddy, I'm so refreshed by the knowledge that God never left me! I know that for sure after my dream today. I just need to discover new ways to communicate with Him now that I reside on the earth. After we leave the womb, our fellowship dynamic changes but not our opportunity to know Him. We can still have relationship with Him if we call out to Him and ask Him to come to us and abide with us. How awesome it is to know that God watches over me and desires to help me no matter what I face.

He truly loves us, Daddy, both in the womb and on the earth. Feeling better today—body, mind, and spirit!

Yours, Brooke

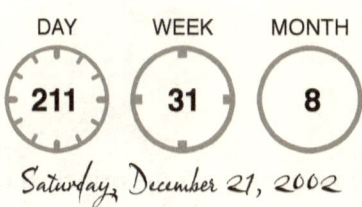

DAY	WEEK	MONTH
211	31	8

Saturday, December 21, 2002

Dear Daddy,

Today has been the best day of my life since being born! Being held by Mommy and you for the first time was awesome. I only wish I could communicate to you both how much it meant to me to feel your embrace and listen to your affectionate words. This was the kind of experience I longed for in the womb—to be held and snuggled by my parents, to be a loved, cherished, involved part of the family. I'll never forget the powerful and longed-for connection this moment brought me.

The agony of waiting for this closeness and being isolated from you behind my plastic secluded world was a big part of what had made my time since birth so difficult. For as long as I can remember, I've longed to be with you and Mommy. My desire to be with you was one of the factors that compelled me to leave the womb early, and it's been a cruel torture that since my birth we've been separated by medical necessity. How good it is to be with you, my parents, even if only for a brief moment! I hope today is the beginning of many special times between us—times of deep connection and rich intimacy. It's hard to wait for the day when I can speak words of love back to you. So for now I'll place them here: I love you Mommy and Daddy! You bring me joy!

I also enjoyed the storybook Mommy read to me. I loved it! That simple little book is true, and just in

case you ever wonder, that's the principal reason I came early—to show you that God, indeed, made me and all His children! God made every human being special, unique, unequalled, and entirely distinct. My purpose is theirs and their purpose is mine: to live, and as we live to have the opportunity to love others and experience this majestic God who made the stars, the canyons, the trees, and, oh, yes, made me!

Just as Mommy's little book speaks, hear me speak, Daddy. Look at me, see who I am; see that I'm fearfully and wonderfully made, see that I'm not something to be discarded, I'm something to be cherished. Hear the children, Daddy! Speak up for those who have not yet acquired a voice that the world can hear. We are made by God, and we bear His image, and we want to live as long as God and this fallen world allows!

Yours, Brooke

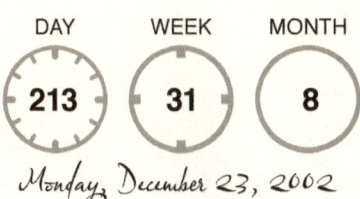

DAY   WEEK   MONTH

213   **31**   **8**

Monday, December 23, 2002

Dear Daddy,

Today was another glorious day! Being held by my grandmothers was a delight. They handled me gingerly and could not get over my size, but they both cared for me, and I could feel their joy at having another grand-child to love. It was a tremendous blessing to be cradled in their arms and sense my connection to the gener-ations of our family. There was a sweetness in their manner—a tenderness, maturity, and wisdom that revealed their experience and years upon the earth.

I was moved by their declarations of love and their prayers. I especially liked hearing that people all over the world were praying for me in various churches and homes. It was a great comfort to know that phone calls had been made and letters and e-mails sent to groups both local and abroad about my birth and medical needs. Hearing that Grandpa was a pastor and that many people around the country were praying for me brought me peace and confidence.

Family is so important, especially in times of crisis or during difficult periods in our lives. I'm glad God instituted it! Surely family plays a vital role in meeting the needs of God's people on earth. A healthy family functioning in the manner in which God intended is a phenomenal blessing. The love, wisdom, provision, and support one gains from family cannot be measured.

I am very grateful to be a part of our family. Being surrounded by the love and care of my grandmothers has brightened my day and left me knowing how richly blessed I am.

I'm still growing, which is good. I heard the doctors say I have grown half an inch since my birth. I'm also glad I don't have to wear the block-out glasses anymore, because my jaundice is under control. My body responded well to the photo-therapy treatments, and it's nice to be able to see again. As time passes, through using my eyes during my little peeks at the world, I am beginning to see with greater clarity and perception. My vision isn't perfect yet, but it's improving. In addition, I'm relieved to have the oxygen tube removed from my nose. The new oxygen hood they replaced it with is so much more comfortable and gives me a greater sense of freedom and independence. Things are definitely getting better, and I'm improving.

I love you, Mom and Dad. I love you, Grandma, Grandpa, and Grams. I wish I could tell you how much your visit and your love means to me more directly than through this diary, but for now it's all I have. I'm hoping you know how I feel by the expression on my face and the rhythm of my heart. Thanks again for your love and care.

Yours, Brooke

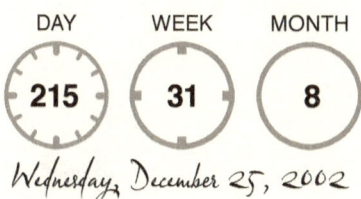

Wednesday, December 25, 2002

Dear Daddy,

My first Christmas was lovely. It was great to be included, as much as possible, in our family's celebration of Christmas. Hearing the Christmas story for the first time in the Bible and in the short storybook version you purchased for me was a treat. I especially liked the account you read from the Gospel of Luke, Daddy. I was amazed to discover that the Son of God came to earth in human form through the womb of His mother, Mary. I was greatly struck by the revelation that Jesus, the King, experienced a similar developmental process to mine and all the other human beings ever created in the history of the world. Perhaps He did it so we could identify with Him and He with us. Every time I encounter Him or learn something new about Him, I'm amazed by Him and His love for people. I suppose there is more to Jesus than one can know. I hope over the course of my life I get to know Him better. I can see from today I have much to learn about Him and so many questions to ask.

My favorite parts of the story were about the angel Gabriel and the meeting between the two mothers, Elizabeth and Mary, and their preborn children, John and Jesus. I wonder if Gabriel was one of the beings I saw when I met with Jesus by the throne. I think some of those beings I saw must have been angels. They certainly were different from people, but also similar.

It must be a great privilege to serve God as an angel, to carry out His assignments, bring good news, and help God's people. Maybe someday in the future I'll see the angels again or meet Gabriel. Just thinking about it gives me chills. How exciting!

As fun as it was to hear about Gabriel, the highlight was the passage that said this:

> When Elizabeth heard Mary's greeting, the baby leaped in her womb; and Elizabeth was filled with the Holy Spirit. And she cried out with a loud voice and said, "Blessed are you among women, and blessed is the fruit of your womb! And how has it happened to me, that the mother of my Lord would come to me? For behold, when the sound of your greeting reached my ears, the baby leaped in my womb for joy. And blessed is she who believed that there would be a fulfillment of what had been spoken to her by the Lord."

Contained in these great words is the validation that preborn children are living persons created, valued, and sent by God for a purpose! Did you hear it as you read it, Daddy? Elizabeth, Mary, John, and Jesus were all at different stages in their journey of life, but they were all wanted, intended, and used for God's glory and purposes.

Hearing how clearly the Bible confirmed the value of every life from conception forward made me wonder how humans with the Bible as a guide could have missed it. How had you and others not heard this truth with clarity, Daddy? Or have people heard it and just chosen to ignore it, or failed to recognize its significance? I'm sensing more than ever the importance of the mission set before me, but mysteries abound. Why, with things being so clear, has the world been led astray? Please, hear the truth, Mommy and Daddy! I've come early to stir you and reveal to you plainly what only appears to be hidden. Look at me! Hear me! Hear also the words of God!

I'm glad you and Mommy celebrate the birth of Jesus. He is truly worthy of celebration and remembrance. I can tell you from my experience with Him, He is the embodiment of love. He certainly is a great gift to humankind, and His gracious gift of life is second to none! Thank you, Mom and Dad, for teaching me about Him, even from the beginning.

Merry Christmas, Brooke

P.S. I like the little toy moose you bought for me. I think it's funny that the moose and I are close to the same size, and I gather from your many comments, so do you. I also like the green Christmas blanket you purchased to cover my protective bubble when I nap. It adds a change of pace to the area I can see in the NICU, giving my surroundings a new hue and glow. Thanks again for loving me and sharing with me the story of Christmas.

DAY	WEEK	MONTH
217	31	8

Friday, December 27, 2002

Dear Daddy,

This morning I'm a little rough around the edges—constipated with a bit of a cough. I know the doctors have expressed some mild concern, but I think I'm going to be fine. I'm just a little out of balance and have a nagging tickle in my throat. But that's the least of my worries. What I really want to share with you is the horrible dream I had earlier this morning. The implications of my latest dream trouble me far more than some momentary constipation. The following is the dream to the best of my remembrance.

The dream started with me alone in a darkened room. A feeling of uneasiness crept over me. Nothing about the place felt secure. As time passed, I felt an impending sense of danger and trepidation as the fear in my heart and mind began to grow. The room was filled with a deadly calm that became more ominous by the minute. I have been afraid before, but I have never, until this dream, felt terrified. Alone in the room, I could sense the danger that was approaching from the outside, and I began to feel great fear build inside of me as the evil approached. While the terror mounted, I began to feel as if I couldn't breathe, and as my panic rose, I nervously started to scream. At first my voice failed, and I only emitted a strained whisper of a sound. However, as my desperate condition became more visceral, I found my voice! Panicked, alone, terrified, and in danger, I screamed for help at the top of my lungs. I shouted and shouted, but no one heard my cries for help. No one came to my aid! As I realized that nothing could protect me from the mounting danger, I began to lose hope and started to hallucinate and worry that I was losing all possession of my mental faculties.

Just when I didn't think I could take a second more of the suspense and terror, I was jolted out of the dream and awoke to find myself short of breath and lying in the NICU. Daddy, I don't know what to make of this dream! I am greatly disturbed by it and afraid for my safety. I don't know if it was a message to me, or a foreshadowing of a breathing problem I'm going to experience when no one at the hospital can help me, or if it's a warning of some kind. I don't have any clarity, but I'm very troubled by it. I have never experienced anything like this before in my dreams. It was so dark and hopeless. I felt a tremendous amount of fear and dread throughout the entire course of the dream.

Needing answers, I'm going to pray and ask God for discernment and protection regarding the dream. I wish that you were here in the NICU with me so I would feel comforted and safe. I know in my mind that God is here with me also, but at times I have difficulty feeling His presence. Please come to me, God, I need Your help!

As I write this, I am reminded of a Scripture you read to me the other day from Isaiah that says, "You are My servant, I have chosen you and not rejected you. Do

not fear, for I am with you; do not anxiously look about you, for I am your God. I will strengthen you, surely I will help you, surely I will uphold you with My righteous right hand."

I don't know how I remember these verses, but I'm glad I do. The Word of God is an incredible comfort to me. I hope you visit me soon, Daddy. Until then, I will place my trust in God.

Yours, Brooke

Saturday, December 28, 2002

Dear Daddy,

I appreciated very much your visit last night and your prayers for me. It brought me great comfort and peace to see you and Mommy, hear your voices, and spend time in your presence. I'm grateful to report that in addition to the comfort of your visit, I received the much needed support I sought from God. You would not believe what happened earlier today if you'd seen it with your own eyes, Daddy. I know this because I saw it with my own eyes, and I can still scarcely comprehend it. The story I'm about to write for you is true and, without a doubt, the most incredible experience of my life thus far.

Last night after you left, I fell into a peaceful sleep, but was jolted out of my sleep in the early morning hours by the same dreadful, dark dream I had the night before. Panicked and short of breath, I cried out in my distress for help. I cried, "Jesus, help me!" At first nothing happened, the NICU and the night nurses seemed as normal as at any other time I have been awake in the night. But then things began to change. My vision, which has been steadily improving, cleared dramatically. It was as clear as when God allowed me to see through the Spirit in the womb. Suddenly, everything in the NICU was clear and plain, without any fuzziness, lack of color, or blur, and descending from above was a glorious being that lit up the room with

his radiant splendor. Thinking he was a messenger from God, I began to relax and anticipate his ministry of help.

As he walked up to me, I noticed that no one else in the NICU could see him but me. He said, "Brooke, I have come to calm your fears and bring you a message from above."

"Who are you?" I asked him.

"I am a prince of God," he replied. He then said, "I've come to interpret your dream. The dark dream you're experiencing is a manifestation of your fears about failing in your mission, of failing to be heard. You're afraid your voice won't be heard, but I have been sent to assure you that people will cheer your name. You will not only be heard, you will be worshiped! God has sent you to testify to life, and that is what you will do as you live gloriously on the earth as a living witness to its beauty and grandeur. However, this isn't just about your voice and your mission, but all voices!"

As he was speaking, I began to smell a slight odor. My sense of smell has come in handy several times since leaving the womb, but today it served me wonderfully. As the smell grew in intensity, it became more repellant. Curiously, he seemed unaware of the odor.

Continuing without recognition, he went on to say, "Every voice is precious, every voice is given equal weight to be heard, and, therefore, you must not violate the voice of anyone else, even if it seems to go against what you came to show and share. You simply need to demonstrate to the people the value of every celebrated life, every wanted child, but you must also give room for others to see things differently. God wants you to be a shining example of the joy-filled life, but he doesn't want you to oppose in any way the choices others make. Through your goodness, tolerance, and example others will learn the truth and celebrate life!"

Interrupting him, I said, "I will not listen to your lies, Satan. I have heard the definitive voice of God regarding life, and I know it's you who wants to withhold choice, squelch voices, murder and deceive people, and convince the world that certain people are unworthy of life and unwanted!"

At this, he shrieked and hissed a most horrible sound and manifested his true visage. Gone was the light, and the true terror of his ugliness was revealed. Angrily, he lashed out toward me and proclaimed, "I'm going to kill you!"

Terrified and desperate, I cried out, "Jesus, help me!" Instantly the room exploded in a blinding wash of light, and heat and Satan was blown to the ground by the force of His coming.

Gathering himself, Satan screamed out in anger, "I have authority here, Lamb of God, you have no right to interfere!"

To which Jesus responded, "All authority in heaven and on earth has been given to Me! It is not the child's time. Now, be gone, Satan, and do not come back!"

Fleeing, the Devil hissed, "This isn't over!"

Turning to me, Jesus said, "My child, I'm so glad

you recognized the Enemy and held fast to the truth. Press forward in faith! He will not return, but nevertheless, there are many who do his bidding, so I will call one of My faithful servants to protect you." Raising His eyes to heaven He said, "Father, holy is Your name. If it pleases You, send the warrior, Hillel, to watch over Brooke. O, righteous Father, thank You for Your goodness."

As Jesus finished His prayer, the angel Hillel appeared. Looking at me, Jesus said, "My child, Hillel will watch over you and stand guard. Now take some rest." After I thanked Jesus for helping me, He departed and the NICU, quiet and calm, came back into view. It was then that I once again realized that none of the night nurses, doctors, or fellow premature infants had witnessed the miraculous exchange!

Only I, through the Spirit of God, can see Hillel. He is huge, Daddy. He must be at least 10 feet tall. If it weren't for the love that emanates from his being, he would be very intimidating. I know I'll be safe with him at my side. I hope that soon you will comprehend my testimony about the preciousness of life in the womb! Hear me, Daddy, there is much at stake! Today's events have clarified for me the stakes of my mission. I must fight on, emboldened after witnessing afresh the power of God!

Rescued, Brooke

P.S. Hillel confirmed that the terrible dream I experienced the last two nights was a nightmare sent by the Devil to terrify me and lead me astray. He assured me I would not experience the dream or its negative consequences in the future. Ironically, Hillel pointed out that the fear and desperation I felt in the nightmare parallel the experience of preborn babies moments before they are killed in the womb. It is clearer than ever that Satan is behind this terrible practice. How horrible this tragedy is, Daddy. The Enemy has deceived humankind through a great ruse. The world is in desperate need of God's truth, illumination, rescue, and forgiveness.

DAY   WEEK   MONTH

220   **32**   **8**

Monday, December 30, 2002

Dear Daddy,

I am praying for you to come to me! I know you were already here this evening, but I need you! Come pray with me in the lateness of the hour. Hillel is locked in a desperate battle with the Enemy's servant, Rawsakh, and it looks as though he may be overcome. Hear me, Daddy! Please hear me, Daddy, come and pray!

Daddy's here...you're really here!

Thank You, Jesus, for allowing my Daddy to hear my petition and come to me in the midnight hour. Daddy, I believe through the Spirit you can hear me. I know you sense something is desperately wrong. Read the Bible and pray, Daddy! Pray with me that God will triumph over the enemy and that the demonic power, Rawsakh, will be overcome.

I hear your prayers, Daddy. Prayers that the Enemy will not triumph over me and that the Lord's grace will be sufficient for me. As you read 1 Peter 4:7-11 and prayed, Rawsakh fell back, and Hillel began to retake the ground he'd lost. I heard the massive demon say, "Just as you are no match for me, Hillel, this weak, sinful man will certainly not affect the outcome by his puny prayers!" Hillel responded, "Listen to the words of God, Rawsakh. They are sharper than any sword! As for this sinner, he's been saved by grace, and he can do all things through Christ who strengthens him!"

After hearing these words, the rebellious one began to curse and swing his giant club with wild abandon. Hillel deflected as many blows as he could with his sword, but alas, a final huge blow from the demon struck the gallant angel and sent him tumbling across the floor. Turning his attention on me, Rawsakh, with great pleasure on his face, exclaimed, "Now you will die, little one!" Scrambling to his feet, Hillel shouted, "The Lord Jesus rebuke you!" Instantly, the bloodthirsty demon was hurled to the floor and began sliding out of view.

* * * * *

Daddy, time has somehow slowed and been suspended as I write this, enabling me to watch and record this epic battle unfolding before me like a dream. Able to see two dimensions at the same time, I can see you sitting by my side praying and reading the Bible as well as the battle between Hillel and Rawsakh, which is happening in the spiritual realm right before my eyes. How and why God is allowing me to experience this I cannot tell, but it is the most exhilarating and terrifying experience of my life! I, like you, Daddy, can only hope and pray. Trusting in God, I will continue to record what happens here as long as I can.

Hillel, exhausted and prayerful, has resumed his defensive position in front of me while you continue to pray. You should see him, Daddy! Hillel is strong

and tall, majestic and alert, adorned with great armor and a mighty sword. His sword is something to behold. The blade has the strength and rigidity of the strongest metal or rock, but it is made up entirely of the elements of water and fire. The core of the sword is pure water that flows like a stream, and the edge is aglow with hot, licking flame.

He has fought valiantly, Daddy, but his enemy is massive. The demonic power, Rawsakh, is almost as wide as he is tall, carrying a twisted and knotted club as hard as a diamond. His weapon is covered with filthy, wet, muddy earth and dried and fresh blood. He is a glutton and a gorger, and it appears he's never satisfied with his lust for blood. Like his master before him, he reeks of filth and death!

Something is happening, Daddy! I hear a deep roar of rage coming from the darkness. Pray hard, Daddy, for Rawsakh is charging Hillel! Rushing to meet the demonic power, Hillel thrusts his sword at the towering demon. As their weapons meet, fire sparks and blood flows! With each blow, the angel prays and the demon curses. As they struggle, I can hear them both speak in languages I cannot understand. In the midst of fierce hand-to-hand fighting, Hillel is starting to lose ground to the humongous demonic force that opposes him.

The tide is turning against Hillel, and I am beginning to feel afraid that the end is near. Once more, I notice you praying beside me. I hear you say, "Lord, Jesus, rescue my precious daughter, Brooke, from the power of the Enemy and give her rest and healing.

Honor Your Word and deliver her from any sickness, oppression, or death. Please, God, hear our prayers for we have little strength, but through Your righteousness and strength, we will prevail in the mighty name of Jesus." As you open my little Bible, tears fall from your eyes as you begin to read from the Psalms:

Behold, the eye of the Lord is on those who fear Him, on those who hope for His lovingkindness, to deliver their soul from death and to keep them alive in famine. Our soul waits for the Lord; He is our help and our shield. For our heart rejoices in Him, because we trust in His holy name. Let Your lovingkindness, O Lord, be upon us, according as we have hoped in You.

I watch intensely as your tears speed across the floor of the NICU and into the core of Hillel's sword. Gathering strength from the words of God, Hillel flips over the giant demon and thrusts his sword through the middle of his club. Staring in amazement, I see the water absorb all the blood and the fire lick up the mud, making the wet dirt hard and brittle. Then as Hillel withdraws his blade, the club shatters and the demon lets out a shriek of pain and rage as he flees from our presence! The battle is over, and the angel has won.

⚹ ⚹ ⚹ ⚹ ⚹

After finishing your prayers and reading the Psalms, you must have sat with me for another 30

minutes. Sensing the danger had passed, you told me goodnight and that you loved me before you departed in the early hours of the morning. Your prayers accomplished more than you know, Daddy. Thank you for praying for me and for coming to visit me in my time of distress. I love you!

Thankful, Brooke

DAY   WEEK   MONTH

224   32   8

Friday, January 3, 2003

Dear Daddy,

I'm happy to report that the demon has not returned and that victory has been achieved! It's been three weeks since my birth, but I now know conclusively that you have made the connection between my premature birth and the grave cost of abortion. I feel a great sense of relief and accomplishment that my plan to be born early has moved your heart to the point of connection.

Earlier today, I received the good news during Uncle Charlie's visit to the NICU. As you both stood over me, I heard you say, "Can you believe we abort these children in America? Look at her! She is so lovely and beautifully formed. Her fingers and her toes are so exquisite, and she's still more than eight weeks from a full term delivery. How on earth can we believe that these children in the womb aren't human beings?"

To which your brother responded, "I know, it's absolutely criminal!"

Seeing me without the veil of the womb worked, you both understood the truth that children in the womb are full human persons. The truth that we are all living human beings from the moment God decides to create us! I'm ecstatic that your ears have opened, Daddy, and that you can hear the voice of the preborn. Please don't forget what you voiced today, and do

whatever you can to champion life in the womb and bring about the ending of abortion!

Thank You, God, for allowing me to be a living testimony to my Daddy and his brother. Lord, use my life to awaken the world to the value of every person, every created life. Nothing on earth matters more than life and the witness it brings of You, the Life-Giver. Thanks again for allowing me the privilege of opening my Daddy's eyes and touching his heart!

Celebrating, Brooke

P.S. You and your brother sound alike. I enjoyed very much meeting him and his wife, Susan. They seem like wonderful people, and I'm glad they're a part of my extended family.

DAY   WEEK   MONTH

227   33   8

Monday, January 6, 2003

Dear Daddy,

I was saddened this morning by a conversation I overheard in the NICU. Two people were looking at a peer of mine and commenting on how hopeless his condition seemed to be. Overwhelmed by his apparent suffering, one of them said, "It would be better if he would just die, or better yet if he had never been born."

The other person responded, "Sometimes abortion is the best option, the most merciful thing."

Appalled, I thought to myself, "These people don't know God, the purpose for life, and the power He possesses! No life is without value, purpose, and possibility! I know God has a plan for this child, weak and hurting as he seems to be, and that He will orchestrate His plan for the good of all, even if we are slow to perceive it." Even in death, if that is what God allows, God is good, and who can tell but what this child will taste as he enters eternity! How dare we say that anyone should never have been born!

I don't know if the individuals I overheard speaking were nurses, doctors, visitors, or family members, but I know they desperately needed to hear the truth that every life is precious, regardless of function or faculty and that God created them, wants them, loves them, and will provide for them, now and forever through His justice and grace. Oh, Daddy, the world is in the dark

when it comes to understanding God's purposes and plans, the role of the Enemy, and the corruption of the earthly realm because of sin. We desperately need God's illumination, vision, and Word.

I hope I have the opportunity to share with the people of the earth the things God has entrusted to me. I want them to know that God is the giver of all life, both temporal and eternal, and that what He has commanded to be, no one should deride or disparage. Human beings, the crown jewel of God's creation, are more than they seem and so much more than any one person could know. Only God knows the whole truth, and, as such, we should trust Him. He knows how we are formed and what we have suffered, and He intends it for good in His timing. Why can't we hear His words and believe His teachings? The Bible says, "His word is a lamp unto our feet and a light unto our path." And again it says, "Trust in the Lord with all your heart and do not lean on your own understanding. In all your ways acknowledge Him, and He will make your paths straight. Do not be wise in your own eyes; fear the Lord and turn away from evil. It will be healing to your body and refreshment to your bones." Daddy, when will we value life?

Disturbed but not deterred, Brooke

Thursday, January 9, 2003

Dear Daddy,

My energy is growing, and my spirit is refreshed listening to all the laughter about me. You and Mommy are having such a good time with some visiting parents and the nurses on duty today. The sound of your hearty laughter and teasing is lifting my burdens and refreshing several other weary souls. The joy of living is so acute during times of celebration and revelry. In the midst of the light-hearted banter, I find myself delighted and grateful to be here with you all. What a joy it is to be in relationship and fellowship with one another. Certainly, one of God's greatest gifts to the human race is fellowship, friends, and family.

I was pleased to hear the news that my cousin, Nathan, was born today in Reno. It will be great fun to have cousins and siblings my own age, or close to my own age, to play with and enjoy life with. God is good, and His blessings are new every morning. Separated by only a few months, it's fun to realize that Nathan and I were both living in the womb at the same time like Jesus and His cousin, John. Happy Birthday, Nathan! Today, I celebrate you along with our entire family. Feeling a special connection with you, I can't wait to meet you in person.

Speaking of celebrations, I'm equally as giddy about the latest update from the doctor. He said, and I

quote, "She's passed the 3-pound marker and is growing quite nicely." My oxygen needs keep diminishing, and my intraventricular hemorrhage is slowly but steadily dissipating. Not to mention, I'm now 17 inches long with the nurse's stretch. I'm feeling better than I have at any other time since my birth. I'm so excited for the future and all it will bring. It's great to be alive, on the mend, and moving forward full of hope and promise.

Who could have guessed my life would be so full of adventure and so grand? I know the future holds even better things for me, and I hope I can accomplish great things with my life. Enjoying the laughter and living in the moment.

Yours, Brooke

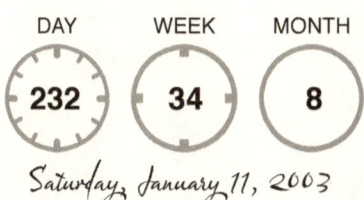

DAY   WEEK   MONTH

232   **34**   **8**

Saturday, January 11, 2003

Dear Daddy,

Wicked Rawsakh is back! This morning he attacked Hillel without warning and without hesitation. Slipping behind Hillel as a dark vapor, Rawsakh manifested himself and sliced off the breastplate of the angel. Whirling to face his foe, Hillel then blocked the death blow of the demon with his sword. In the clash, I noticed that Rawsakh's new club was much smaller than it had been during their first confrontation. Strangely, though, as they exchanged blows, Rawsakh's club visibly grew in size and power. Something was feeding his power. As they fought in a vicious struggle, blood flowed from the blunt, gnarled instrument that Rawsakh employed in his attack.

Falling back under the fierceness of the assault, I heard Hillel say, "Lord, Jesus, give me strength!" Then he ducked a massive swinging blow of the enemy and simultaneously contacted Rawsakh squarely in the chest, sending the giant demon skidding backward with great force. Taking up a position in front of me, Hillel bowed his head, uttered a silent prayer, and began to sing. In mid-charge, with his club raised high over his head, Rawsakh fell to his knees, dropped his weapon, covered his ears, and began gnashing his teeth as Hillel sang!

Turning my attention to Hillel, I heard the sound of his beautiful voice. Smiling and appearing as if arrayed

in a rainbow of colors, I heard him sing, "Holy, Holy, Holy, are You, Jehovah! There is none like You. You are the glorious One, and I will forever praise You. Out of the grave You rose to rule, victorious over all Your foes. There is no one like You . . ."

Looking back at Rawsakh, I noticed he had started to burn and scream from the effects of Hillel's glorious song of worship and praise. Not able to stand Hillel's abandon to God, he limped off and faded in the distance.

Hillel continued to worship for a time, and then, falling prostate and exhausted, he gave thanks to God. Praying in a language I did not understand, he regained his strength and then walked the perimeter of the NICU to make sure Rawsakh had departed and I was safe.

When he returned, I asked the angel why the demon had been so affected by his worship of God.

Hillel said, "Brooke, the demonic forces of the world through their rebellion have lost the ability to love God. They can't stand it when anyone chooses of their own free will to praise the Creator and extol His greatness. They typically flee from a worshiping heart."

I then asked him, "Why was Rawsakh's club growing during the fight?"

He replied, "Rawsakh is strengthened and empowered by the shedding of innocent blood. The greater the number of innocents that are sacrificed, the more powerful he becomes."

Saddened, I stopped asking questions and thanked the angel for his worship and intercession on my behalf.

My heart hurts, Daddy. When will the people of the earth wake up and stop participating with the demons in the slaughter of their children? I feel weakened and drained from this latest attack of the Enemy.

Protected, Brooke

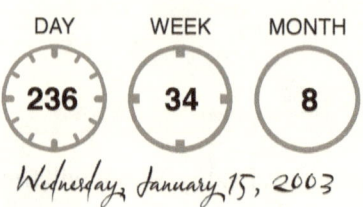

DAY **236**   WEEK **34**   MONTH **8**

Wednesday, January 15, 2003

Dear Daddy,

All the recent excitement has left me out of breath, literally. Yesterday the doctors put me back on the oxygen tube that goes in my nose. I must admit I've been experiencing more breathing struggles lately. I'm disappointed by the development, but it's probably a good thing. Since being on it, I feel refreshed and my energy level is growing. I'm sure in no time at all I'll be back to normal without the aid of the oxygen tube.

It's been hard to adjust to you and Mommy's return to work. I'd grown fond of your visits during the day, and now I have to wait until the evening to spend time with you. As I contemplated how much time you and Mommy have spent here with me, it got me thinking about who takes care of Elijah when you are both in the NICU with me. It must be hard at times to juggle visits to the hospital, work, and family needs. I hope you sense that I value you both so much! All your hard work, care, and prayers are greatly appreciated. I love you, Mommy and Daddy, and I realize you love me and care for me. Besides, I'm not really alone. I know Jesus is always watching over me, and I have Hillel as my constant companion, especially now that he's finished construction on his perimeter of light.

You should see it, Daddy! It's a towering wall of light that wraps the NICU like a castle moat. A fascinating device, it allows Hillel to see the deeds, thoughts, and intentions of anyone who passes through the barrier. I didn't realize until recently that most of the nights I've been asleep, Hillel has been battling the Enemy's servant on the perimeter of the NICU. He has worked relentlessly, and I can see the evidence of fatigue upon his face. I thought his wall of light was a marvelous early detection device, but Hillel explained it was protective, as well. He said, "Brooke, the Enemy hates the light, and his demon will not come to it easily for it will expose his deeds, the depravity of his heart, and the sinfulness of his condition. The light will pose a strong deterrent to Rawsakh's coming because he bears great iniquity." I found this telling and comforting. Maybe now the Enemy will give up his assault and his attempts to take my life!

I hope Mommy will read to me this evening like she normally does. I especially like the children's storybook about Easter. I love the story of Jesus' resurrection from the dead. I'm grateful that Jesus holds the power over death, and I can tell you from experience He is very much alive!

Yours, Brooke

DAY	WEEK	MONTH
238	34	8

Friday, January 17, 2003

Dear Daddy,

The last couple of days have been very restful, and, as a result, I'm no longer using the oxygen tube. I feel stronger and more energized. I think I'm about to turn yet another corner in my health and take some giant steps toward my release from the hospital.

Being able to relax because of Hillel's latest defenses has helped tremendously with my progress and peace. I realized today that I failed to mention, over the last couple of weeks, my ability to see with clarity. Ever since the confrontation between Jesus and Satan, I have had the ability to see with perfect perception, color, and clarity. I love looking in Mommy's face when she's holding me, especially now that I can see without limitation. I can even make out the words "Daddy" and "Mommy" on the pictures the nurses took of you guys. I like having them taped to my plastic home. I often look at them when you're not here and feel comforted by them.

It's been intense to see with my own eyes the NICU and the spiritual realm of angels and demons. I love seeing naturally in the same way I was able to see through the Spirit of God in the womb and in my dreams. There are so many other children in the NICU with me—boys and girls of all shapes, skin tones, and sizes. Some of the children are younger than me, and some are older.

Yesterday I heard a doctor say we had a new arrival that was just over a pound in weight and around twenty-four weeks gestation—another testimony to life in the womb, a person every bit as beautiful as the rest of us!

Surrounded by these children, I feel hope for the future. Hope that they will remember their Creator and stand up for the rights of their peers. God said I was one of His witnesses, but surely I'm not alone in this call. I know He's going to send others. Perhaps in this very room or currently residing in the womb are a number of great deliverers who will champion justice and the rights of all humankind: both born and preborn, male and female, young and old. Maybe the world's next great minister is lying here waiting to tell the world about Jesus' love, or perhaps a gifted neonatal doctor, teacher, poet, scholar, or reformer. I can only guess, but I know life is precious and its potential is limitless. Our time in the womb is the foundation, the beginning point, upon which everything else in our lives will be built. I hope and pray that the human race will come to its senses and heed the truth about human life, human worth, and its preciousness from creation forward.

Hopeful, Brooke

DAY	WEEK	MONTH
241	35	9

Monday, January 20, 2003

Dear Daddy,

I'm very happy today! My breathing has improved to the point where the doctors have cleared me to be moved to an open-air crib. No more barriers! I can begin to enjoy life like an ordinary infant. This is very exciting as it will allow me to be closer to you and Mommy when you visit. I'm also proud to disclose that at this morning's weigh-in, I checked in at a handsome 4 pounds, 3 ounces! Not only that, but I've reached 17½ inches in length, pretty good for a little girl who started out as a tiny single cell. Surely I'm well on my way to being released from the hospital and coming home.

As happy as I am about my physical improvements, I'm even happier about my latest dream. I woke up this morning aglow with the joy of victory and hope. I want to share it with you, Daddy. It's a beautiful dream!

It began with me walking down a sunlit path. The radiant beams of light danced on my feet and made my skin feel ecstatic. The path was lined with beautiful trees, shrubs, and flowers that gave off the most alluring and pleasant aroma. At several points along my journey, I stopped to behold the colors of the foliage and take in the beauty of the path. Walking further, I felt a slight breeze began to blow on my face and ruffle my hair as I approached a magnificent garden. Nearing the garden, I heard laughter and singing. An immaculate greenbelt was alive with anticipation, activity, and play. A group of children had filled the garden to overflow, and it seemed the boys and girls gathered there were excitedly nervous—happy, but clearly not quite sure what to expect or how to conduct themselves.

Watching with wonder and anticipation, I settled down near a babbling stream and a giant shade tree to observe the spectacle. One by one, I noticed the children were being summoned by a glorious angel. When a child's name was announced, they would approach the angel and leave the garden through a tunnel of lilacs and flowers. Turning my attention to some children close to me, I heard one of them say, "I'm so nervous; what is it going to be like? What am I going to say to them? I hope it's the right thing; I've dreamed of this day all my life!"

To which one of her peers responded, "Relax, it's going to be wonderful. I got to meet my dad for the first time three years ago, and it was one of the best moments of my life, and today I get to be reunited with my mom, a glorious answer to all my prayers for her."

It was then that I noticed that the young man who was talking was the same person who had come to me in an earlier dream and shown me his mother in a desperate struggle for life. Looking more closely at his face to make sure he was the person I had met earlier, I said, "Hi, I'm Brooke; do you remember me?"

"Sure I do; you're one of God's witnesses," he answered. As I started to ask him some more questions, his name was called, and he grabbed my hand and said, "Come, see for yourself!"

Overwhelmed by his graciousness, I followed him swiftly through the tunnel of flowers. Exiting the tunnel, I saw a magnificent pool of flowing water surrounded by flowers the likes of which I'd never seen. The beauty in this part of the garden was unparalleled and glorious. Standing by the pool with a flower in her hand was his elegant mother—just as lovely as I remembered her. Not wanting to interfere more than I already had, I stepped against the foliage at the edge of the tunnel and said, "Thank you for inviting me, but I shall come no further." Turning from me with gratitude, I watched as he approached his mother.

Fading from that place, I found myself standing in a sea of celebrating adults and children, with the children composing by far the larger number. Mesmerized, I stood and beheld the people. Their joy was contagious as they danced, leapt, and embraced. In the ruckus, I asked the person standing to my right in the loudest voice I could muster, "What's going on? What are you celebrating?"

"The people of America have decided to end the legalized practice of abortion in their land!" she joyfully shouted.

Undone, I closed my eyes, listened to the shouts of joy, and thanked God for His mercy. Standing there with a feeling of satisfaction I cannot describe, I awoke in the NICU with renewed hope and a taste of the victory yet to come.

Encouraged, Brooke

Just when I thought my day couldn't get any better, it has! Your visit has topped off my day and brought me sublime satisfaction. I love the new blanket you and Mommy picked out for me to use in my new crib. It's so soft and beautiful. I was so delighted to be held by you and Mommy this afternoon. I could tell your excitement over my recent progress is as great as mine. You both seemed happy and relieved. I feel so much joy today, I can hardly contain it.

The surprise visit of Elijah, however, took it over the top! Seeing my brother for the first time as you held him up to the glass was the highlight of my week. He's so young and handsome. I wish you could bring him inside the NICU, but I've gathered young children are not allowed. Still, it was great to see him and make a connection with him.

I wish the nurse would have held me up longer, but I guess it was a little awkward with my wires and all. It's been a great day, Daddy, the best of my life thus far.

Joyful, Brooke

DAY 242   WEEK 35   MONTH 9

Tuesday, January 21, 2003

Dear Daddy,

My heart is breaking! In the early hours of the morning, Rawsakh and a monstrous demon named Zawnaw attacked Hillel's defenses with wild abandon. The terror I experienced as they crossed the barrier of light sent my oxygen demands through the roof and caused a great shock to pulse through my body. What I saw with my eyes I will not record, for I believe no one should have to relive it, but I will tell you that the screams of Rawsakh's victims were the most horrible, lamentable sounds imaginable. The demonic power Zawnaw also manifested many exceedingly wicked and sordid things. Hillel has fought courageously with a combination of Scripture, worship, prayer, and sword play, but the two powers have maintained a relentless attack. Many times they've pressed their advantage to the edge of my crib—close enough to touch me. But each time, Hillel has repelled them with a dazzling display of courage, faith, and power.

Despite all of Hillel's valor, my body is breaking! I don't know if it is the load of stress that my immune system cannot handle or if it is something the demons have effected, but I am in trouble, Daddy. The doctors rushed to my aid around mid-morning and had to revive me out of shock and arrest. Again this afternoon after more intense attacks from the enemy, I needed to be kept from death by the excellent medical team in the

NICU. Finally, in an awesome display of bravery using the Words of God and precise agility, Hillel was able to rout the enemy and drive them past the perimeter of light and into the darkness. The damage is great, however, and I feel I won't last for long.

Come to me, my parents, and stay with me. I pray God will give me the strength to be with you one last time on earth. I love you, Mommy and Daddy, please come to me. Come to me in my distress! Jesus, let my parents hear me that they may come to me.

Wounded, Brooke

Thank You, Jesus, for allowing my parents to come to me in my greatest hour of need and encourage my soul with Your Word. Thank you for reading Hebrews 11:1 and Ephesians 6:10-18 to me, Mommy. Thank you for reading 1 Peter 5:7-11, Psalm 139, Revelation 22:17, and Psalm 23 to me, Daddy. I'll love you always, and I'll wait for you in heaven.

I'm going to close my final entry with Psalm 139. My heart is breaking literally and spiritually because of the Enemy of life. Hear these Words, peoples of the earth, and rest not until abortion is defeated and this reign of death is cast down:

> O Lord, You have searched me and known me.
> You know when I sit down and when I rise up;
> You understand my thought from afar.

You scrutinize my path and my lying down,
And are intimately acquainted with all my ways.
Even before there is a word on my tongue,
Behold, O Lord, You know it all.
You have enclosed me behind and before,
And laid Your hand upon me.
Such knowledge is too wonderful for me;
It is too high, I cannot attain to it.
Where can I go from Your Spirit?
Or where can I flee from Your presence?
If I ascend to heaven, You are there;
If I make my bed in Sheol, behold, You are there.
If I take the wings of the dawn,
If I dwell in the remotest part of the sea,
Even there Your hand will lead me,
And Your right hand will lay hold of me.
If I say, "Surely the darkness will overwhelm me,
And the light around me will be night,"
Even the darkness is not dark to You,
And the night is as bright as the day.
Darkness and light are alike to You.
For You formed my inward parts;
You wove me in my mother's womb.
I will give thanks to You, for I am fearfully and
    wonderfully made;
Wonderful are Your works,
And my soul knows it very well.

My frame was not hidden from You,
When I was made in secret,
And skillfully wrought in the depths of the earth;
Your eyes have seen my unformed substance;
And in Your book were all written
The days that were ordained for me,
When as yet there was not one of them.
How precious also are Your thoughts to me, O
    God!
How vast is the sum of them!
If I should count them, they would outnumber the
    sand.
When I awake, I am still with You.
O that You would slay the wicked, O God;
Depart from me, therefore, men of bloodshed.
For they speak against You wickedly,
And Your enemies take Your name in vain.
Do I not hate those who hate You, O Lord?
And do I not loathe those who rise up against You?
I hate them with the utmost hatred;
They have become my enemies.
Search me, O God, and know my heart;
Try me and know my anxious thoughts;
And see if there be any hurtful way in me,
And lead me in the everlasting way.

Letters to My Dad

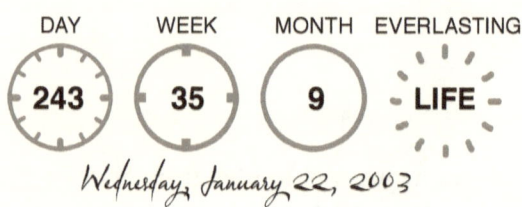

DAY   WEEK   MONTH EVERLASTING

243   35   9   LIFE

Wednesday, January 22, 2003

Dear Daddy,

God permitted me one last entry to you from the shores of heaven. Do not be dismayed, Daddy, my life was not in vain. I fulfilled my purpose. Your little stream full of grace and mercy accomplished her mission. Go forward and spread the message of life, defend the least of these in the womb and the hurting, rescue the lost and those scarred by abortion. Today on this thirtieth observance of the tragic Roe v Wade decision, remember the cost to our nation and plead with other believers to take a stand against the demonic stronghold of abortion through prayer, fasting, repentance, and action. Follow God's ways and seek Him, and He will make your paths straight.

Daddy, do you remember my first dream in the womb about the little girl and her father playing chase? It's me! I'm living that dream this very day with my Father in heaven. Weep not for me, for I am in the loveliest place with the most magnificent, adoring God. Daddy, nothing can separate us from His love if we trust Him!

If you and Mommy are ever sad or discouraged by my passing, read Psalm 121. The Psalm not only marks the day of my arrival in heaven, but it marks the fulfillment of your hopes for me and God's promise of provision to me. Remember, Daddy, God brings life out of death! And I can assure you, Jesus is everything He said He is! I love you, my family, with all my heart, and God loves you even more. He loves with an everlasting love.

Yours forever, Brooke

P.S. Tell Mommy the exhausted angel she saw at my passing was not a figment of her imagination—it was Hillel. When Jesus called my name and I left my body, Hillel gathered me in his arms, unfurled his wings, and rushed me to the Prince of Peace!

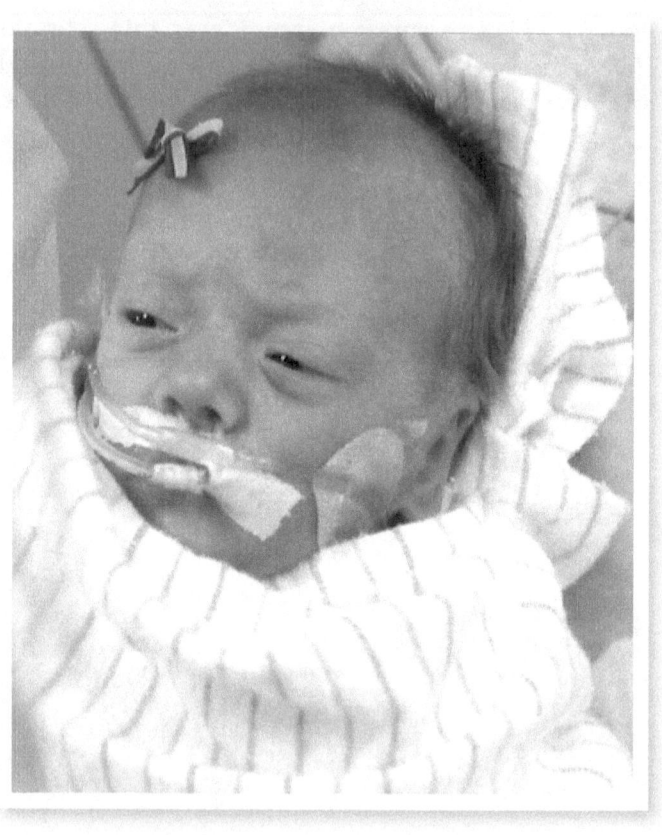

Brooke Anna Vaughan Patchen
January 2003

Afterword

Following Brooke's death, two memorial services were held in her honor. On January 28, 2003, her body was laid to rest in Denver, Colorado, my home state. Knowing full well Brooke's soul was not there, her mother and I inscribed the words "Safe with Jesus" and the Scripture reference Isaiah 57:1, 2 on her footstone.

In the years that followed Brooke's death, as I worked through the stages of grief and healing, I contemplated the impact Brooke's life had on me and the challenge it posed to legalized abortion. Deciding adoption was the best alternative to abortion, I began to contemplate a career change and my possible involvement in the field of adoption.

Leaving the teaching profession, I moved my family back to Colorado. After several fruitless efforts to get involved in the adoption industry and a rough stint at a local bank where I was robbed twice, once by a drug addict with a knife and the other by a military-style crew with body armor and M16s, I decided to enter the pro-life field in 2006. Volunteering, I spent the better part of a year working with a local Right-to-Life chapter, primarily in the areas of fund-raising, church outreach, and church recruitment. This was a time of great education, increased awareness, and disappointment. The up-close encounter with the apathy,

ignorance, opposition, and hopelessness I discovered in the many different denominations and branches of Christianity was shocking, painful, and revealing.

As a result of my experience with churches, my year-long education concerning the pro-life and pro-choice movements, and the results of a personal search for the biblical position on life's beginning and purpose, I felt the body of Christ needed to be re-educated on the biblical mandate to rescue the weak, needy, oppressed, poor, and fatherless, as well as the great biblical doctrine on the sanctity of human life. This conviction led me to a season of research and Bible study that culminated in the foundation of a new pro-life ministry and the publication of my first book: *Who Am I? 25 Biblical Reasons Why Christians Should Respect, Honor, Protect, and Defend Human Life!* The book is a comprehensive Bible study on the sanctity of human life, abortion, and the church's responsibility to work tirelessly toward the abolition of legalized abortion in America and the world. Following the book came the incorporation of Anna's Choice, LLC (www.annaschoice.org), a ministry I founded in 2008 with the purpose of equipping and encouraging the body of Christ to take action against the ongoing atrocity of abortion.

The organization proudly derives its name from the powerful witness of my daughter, Brooke, concerning the humanity, dignity, value, and reality of life in the womb. While the story you have just read is fictional, it derives much of its content from real-life experiences during her time in the NICU and the practical and spiritual awakening her life produced in me regarding the horror of abortion, the beauty of fetal development, and life in the womb. Brooke's full name is Brooke Anna Vaughan Patchen, which means "stream full of grace and mercy little Patchen." I believe the ministry of Anna's Choice to the church, the post-abortive, and the oppressed children in the womb is an extension of my daughter's namesake—a little stream full of grace and mercy.

In 2010, I finished writing a daily devotional, *Love is for Eternity*, and, in early 2011, the work you've just finished reading. These works reflect my heart and passion for the pro-life cause and the lessons I've learned through my time with Brooke, study of the Scriptures, and many excellent pro-life resources. I hope and pray that the body of Christ and the rest of America will rise up and challenge the status quo of legalized abortion, bringing our nation back to its founding principles of the right to "Life, Liberty, and the Pursuit of Happiness," rights granted by our Creator without respect to any other consideration except that one be a member of the human race—a right we all enjoy from the first moment God creates us at conception (fertilization).

Aware more every day of the tremendous toll abortion has exacted on its second victim, the post-abortive man or woman, I sincerely hope the ministry of Anna's Choice will also bring forgiveness and healing to the millions of people left with shattered lives, wounded

souls, and physical scars wrought from the lies of abortion. It is my fervent hope that Brooke's story compels you to seek a relationship with Jesus Christ and discover His life-giving water and abundant grace. It's never too late to come to the Life-Giver and let Him mend the breach, renew your mind, forgive your sin, and refresh your soul.

I pray the following Scriptures will encourage you and prove helpful in your healing and recovery. Lamentations 3:22, 23 affirms, "The Lord's lovingkindnesses indeed never cease, for His compassions never fail. *They* are new every morning; great is Your faithfulness." And First John 1:9 assures, "If we confess our sins, He is faithful and righteous to forgive us our sins and to cleanse us from all unrighteousness." May you find peace and many helpful treasures as you explore God's Word and these other recommended Scriptures (Psalms 30:11, 12; 32:1-5; 34:17, 18; 130:3, 4; 147:3; Micah 7:18, 19; John 3:16; 4; 8:1-11; Romans 8; 10:9-13; 2 Corinthians 5:17-21; Titus 3:3-7;1 Peter 2:24; 5:7; Jude 24, 25; Revelation 21:5-7; 22:17).

On behalf of Anna's Choice ministries, I encourage anyone who doesn't know Jesus Christ as Lord and Savior to find a Bible-believing church and search out for yourself His claims and life-giving power. Get a Bible and start reading the New Testament, especially the Gospel of John.

If you feel you are ready to accept Christ's free gift of eternal life today and join Brooke in heaven when your earthly life is through, I invite you to pray the following prayer and then seek out a Bible-believing church to celebrate with you your decision and augment your faith:

Lord Jesus, I believe in You! I know I'm a sinner, and I realize I need You to bear my burden of sin and shame. God, I confess I have trespassed against You, knowingly and unknowingly. Forgive me and take away my sins, giving me a new heart and a new spirit. Jesus, I want to follow You. Please come into my life, bringing Your Holy Spirit, and show me the way to live. Thank You, Lord Jesus, for loving me and paying my sin debt on the cross. Show me how to be Your child and Your disciple. Amen!

Welcome to the family of God! May the Lord richly bless you both now and forever.

If you would like to contact Anna's Choice for additional materials, speaking engagements, or any other purpose, call (719) 651-5335 or contact us through the Web at www.annaschoice.org. You may also contact us by mail or e-mail at: Anna's Choice, P.O. Box 64262, Colorado Springs, CO 80962 or joel@annaschoice.org. God bless you, and thank you for allowing me to share Brooke's story.

Recommended Reading and Selected Resources

Pro-Life Issues

Alcorn, Randy. *Why Pro-Life?*

Brown, Harold O. J. *Death before Birth* (early pro-life call to action)

Ensor, John. *Answering the Call* (loving one's neighbor)

Tallack, Peter. *In the Womb* (embryonic & fetal development)

Willke, John, and Barbara Willke. *Abortion Questions and Answers* (comprehensive abortion Q&A, informative)

Grieving the Loss of a Child

Burpo, Todd, with Lynn Vincent. *Heaven is for Real* (a child's experience with heaven)

Simmons, Eldyn. *The Dawn of Hope* (grieving the loss of a loved one)

Verwys, Mary Waalkes. *Wednesday Mourning* (sidewalk counselor's testimony)

Wiersbe, David. *Gone but Not Lost* (grieving the death of a child)

Christian Theology and Apologetics

Lewis, C. S. *Mere Christianity* (Christian apologetics)

Spurgeon, Charles. *All of Grace* (the grace of God)

Tozer, A. W. *The Knowledge of the Holy* (the attributes of God)

Courage and Faith

Stowe, Harriet Beecher. *Uncle Tom's Cabin* (classic fictional work instrumental in the abolition of chattel slavery in America)

ten Boom, Corrie. *The Hiding Place* (courage and rescue in the face of Nazi persecution)

Wilberforce, William. *Real Christianity* (a discussion of authentic faith)

Books Especially for Children

Lucado, Max. *Just In Case You Ever Wonder* (one of the children's books we read to Brooke)

Seuss, Dr. (Theodor Seuss Geisel), *Horton Hears a Who!* (great story and prolife allegory)

Walburg, Lori. *The Legend of the Candy Cane* (a wonderful Christmas story)

Websites

www.ramahinternational.org (post-abortive recovery)

www.care-net.org (pregnancy resource centers)

www.40daysforlife.com (prayer)

www.abort73.com (informative)

www.pregnantpause.org (informative)

In addition, we encourage you to check out our website, *www.annaschoice.org.* Learn more about Anna's Choice, obtain other books by the author, or purchase the *Who Am I?* Bible study to lead in your church or small group.

Additional Information

Meaning of Hebrew Character Names for Supernatural Beings

Information is from *Strong's Hebrew and Chaldee Dictionary*—James Strong, LL.D., S.T.D., *The New Strong's Exhaustive Concordance of the Bible* (Nashville: Thomas Nelson Publishers, 1990), 33, 35, 110.

Hillel: praising—"Hillel, *hil-layl;*" praising (namely God). See # 1985.

Rawsakh: to dash in pieces, to *murder*—"Ratsach, *raw-tsakh;* to dash to pieces, i.e. kill (a human being), especially to murder: put to death, kill, (man-) slay (-er), murder (-er). See # 7523.

Zawnaw: adultery, fornication, whoredom—"Zanah, *zaw-naw;* a prim. root [highly *fed* and therefore wanton]; to commit adultery; fig. to commit idolatry: (cause to) commit fornication, x continually, x great, (be a, play the) harlot, whoredom." See # 2181.

Developmental Markers

All human developmental markers alluded to in this work were taken from Peter Tallack's book, *In the Womb* (Washington, DC: National Geographic Society, 2006). All times referenced and presented are approximate. For greater detail and fuller descriptions of embryonic and fetal development, refer to Tallack's book or other medical, scientific, and biological sources dealing with human life in the womb. Likewise, all Scriptures quoted, paraphrased, or alluded to in this work were taken from *The Holy Bible, New American Standard Bible*. This is the version of the Bible I purchased for Brooke on the day of her birth.

I have included a few brief excerpts from *In the Womb* along with the diary date for the first eight weeks of human development and some applicable Bible references. Apart from the included quotes, I will only list the page number when referencing Tallack's book.

May 25, 2002: "The tail detaches and the sperm's nucleus is drawn toward the nucleus of the egg. The two nuclei gradually and gracefully become one. Fertilization is complete: Two sets of genetic material, one from the mother, one from the father, combine to make a new genetic message. This is the moment of conception, when an individual's unique set of DNA is created—a human signature that never existed before and will never be repeated" (26).

Bible references: Genesis 1:26-28; 4:1;
     Jeremiah 1:5; Colossians 1:15-20;
     Hebrews 3:4.

May 30, 2002: 34.

June 1, 2002: 36.

June 3, 2002: "By day ten, the still microscopic embryo has disappeared inside the lining of the uterus. . . . Once the embryo is firmly dug in, the trophoblast starts secreting a hormone called human chorionic gonadotrophin. Without this hormone, the lining would break down and menstrual bleeding would begin—a catastrophe for the embryo" (36).

June 7, 2002: 40. "Because the nervous system coordinates the action of most of the body's other systems, it begins to form very early and continues to develop until birth and beyond. By the end of the first month, the embryo will have established the foundation of its entire nervous system" (44).

June 12, 2002: 28.

June 14, 2002: "Its (embryo) primitive neurons will clump together to become nerves and eventually permeate every minute region of the growing body, sending and receiving messages at up to 300 miles per hour" (44).

Bible reference: Hebrews 11:1.

June 16, 2002: "The cardiovascular system is one of the first major systems to start working in the embryo. At this stage the clump of heart cells—about the size of a poppy seed—is still. Arranged initially as a pair of crescent-shaped tracts, these fuse to form a single S-shaped tube, which is plumbed into blood vessels in the embryo, yolk sac, chorion, and connecting stalk to form a basic cardiovascular system. On day 22 or 23, at the start of week 4, single heart cell jolts into life. This tiny movement sparks a chain reaction, and other cells in the cluster pick up the rhythm. The new cells divide, dance to the same beat, and eventually grow into the baby's four-chambered heart" (50).

June 21, 2002: "Day 28...the embryo...is still no bigger than the head of a match, yet all her vital organs are already mapped out" (52).

July 7, 2002: 54.

July 13, 2002: Weeks 7 and 8— "The embryo has all her major organs and body systems in place. . . . The light-sensitive cells of the retina have formed, and nerve connections from the retina to the brain have been established" (56).

Bible reference: Matthew 6:22.

July 18, 2002: "Despite their closeness, there is no direct connection between the two sets of blood vessels in the placenta… The circulations of the mother and fetus are side by side, but they never mix" (62).

"By the eighth week the muscles and nervous system have started to become interconnected and integrated, with the embryo making its first purposeful movements" (56).

July 21, 2002: "The brain is sculpted in a similar but subtler fashion, by the creation of too many cells and the elimination of those that don't fit the required patterns of interconnections. Suicide seems to be part of the developmental deal: death programmed as a tool of life. Programmed cell death helps to keep the number of cells in an organ…within certain limits" (58).

August 2, 2002: 148.

Bible reference: Matthew 11:30.

August 7, 2002: 78 and 82.

Bible references: Job 38:16; Nehemiah 9:6; Job 38:31-33; Psalms 8:1-6; 19:1-4; 89:11; 136:1-9; 147:4, 5; Isaiah 40:12-14; 45:12; Jeremiah 10:12, 13; Habakkuk 3:3, 4; Colossians 1:16, 17; Hebrews 1:10; 2 Peter 3:5.

August 15, 2002: 83.

August 19, 2002: 86.

Bible references: Genesis 1:26; 1; Psalm 33:6-9;
Colossians 1:15-20; Hebrews 3:3, 4;
Deuteronomy 31:8.

August 21, 2002: 88, 90.

August 27, 2002: 100.

Bible references: Genesis 21:2; Ecclesiastes 3:1-8;
Acts 17:23-31.

September 1, 2002: 148.

September 6, 2002: 96.

Bible references: Genesis 1:26, 27; 2;
Deuteronomy 10:12-15; Psalm 145; Proverbs
8:17, 36; Micah 6:8; 7:18; Zephaniah 3:17;
Matthew 5:43-48; 22:35-40; John 13:35;
15:9-17; 17:17-26; Romans 5:8-21; 13:8-11; 1
Corinthians 13; 1 John 4:7-21.

September 11, 2002: 32, 94.

September 15, 2002:

Bible references: Job 31:15; Genesis 3;
Deuteronomy 30:15-20; 1 Chronicles 29:11;
Psalm 73; 19; Isaiah 6:3; Matthew 28:16-20;
John 16:7-15; 17; Romans 1:19, 20; John 5:24;
2 Timothy 1:10; 2 Samuel 14:14; John 14:6.

Additional Bible references: John 10:9-11; Acts 4:9-12; Matthew 7:7; James 1:5; Jeremiah 1:5; Galatians 1:11-16; Isaiah 43:10-13.

September 21, 2002: 94, 142.

September 24, 2002:

Bible references: Deuteronomy 29:29; Genesis 5; Psalm 90:10; Romans 6:23; Jeremiah 19:4; Romans 9:10-12; Deuteronomy 10:17, 18; 2 Samuel 12:22, 23; Psalm 10:10-14; Matthew 18:14; Luke 18:15-17.

October 3, 2002: 82, 86.

October 8, 2002: 116, 118.

October 13, 2002: Original song, "Jesus Loves Me" by Anna B. Warner and William B. Bradbury, in Robert J. Morgan, Then Sings My Soul: 150 of the World's Greatest Hymn Stories (Nashville, TN: Thomas Nelson, 2003), 138, 139.

October 17, 2002: 78, 86, 104, 120, 122, 130.

October 25, 2002: 148, 149.

Bible references: Psalms 37:18; 89:47, 48; 90:12; 103:14-19; Ecclesiastes 3:1, 2, 11-15; 9:11, 12; Romans 8:18-23; Ephesians 5:15-17; James 4:13-15.

November 4, 2002:

> Bible references: Psalms 127:3, 4; 128;
> Proverbs 17:6.

November 7, 2002:

> Bible references: Deuteronomy 1:21; Psalm 27:1;
> Ecclesiastes 11:4; 2 Timothy 1:7.

November 13, 2002:

> Bible reference: Jeremiah 33:22.

November 17, 2002: 108, 114, 116.

November 27, 2002:

> Bible references: Jeremiah 1:6-8; 25:4; Ezekiel
> 3:10; Zechariah 7:9-12; Mark 4:19-23;
> 2 Corinthians 12:2-4; Numbers 24:4;
> Psalms 11:4; 97:2; Isaiah 6:1-8; Ezekiel 1; 2; 3;
> 16:20-22; Daniel 7:9-14; 8:17; Matthew 25:31;
> Luke 13:34; Romans 8:26, 34; Hebrews 2:11-
> 18; 4:14-16; 8:1; Revelation 1:10-18; 4;
> 2 Chronicles 7:14; Psalms 37:27, 28; 68:19,
> 20; Proverbs 24:10-12; Joel 2:12-14; Micah
> 7:18, 19; Matthew 18:12-14; Luke 18:1-8;
> John 10:27-30; 17.

December 1, 2002: 108, 110, 114, 124, 130, 148, 149.

December 5, 2002:

> Bible references: Job 3:11-19; Psalm 10:14;
> Jeremiah 20:17.

December 9, 2002: 110, 134.

December 12, 2002:

Bible references Isaiah 6:8; Genesis 3; Isaiah 25:8, 9; John 9:1-12; Romans 5:12-17; Revelation 21:4.

Additional Bible references: Genesis 3:1-5, 14, 15; Deuteronomy 32:17, 18; 1 Chronicles 21:1, 14; Job 1; 2; Psalm 106:36-38; Matthew 16:23; Mark 5:1-17; Luke 9:38-43; 13:10-17; 22:31; John 8:44; Acts 10:38; Ephesians 6:11, 12; 2 Thessalonians 2:9; Hebrews 2:14, 15; 1 Peter 5:8; 1 John 3:8; Revelation 2:13; 6:9; 9:11, 14, 15; 12:3, 4, 9; 18:2; Psalms 55:16; 86:11; 119:160; 141:1; 145:18; Isaiah 45:19; Jeremiah 33:3; John 1:14; 17:17; 18:37; Deuteronomy 31:6; 1 Kings 8:57; 1 Chronicles 28:20; Hebrews 13:5.

December 15, 2002:

Bible reference Isaiah 43:1-4.

December 20, 2002:

Bible references: John 4:10-15; Matthew 16:24, 25; 23:11, 12; Mark 10:21; John 12:24-26; 15:18-21; Philippians 2:3-11; 1 Peter 2:19-24 1 Chronicles 16:11; Isaiah 55:6; John 14:16-18; 15:1-17; Acts 17:27; James 4:8; 1 John 2:27; 4:11-15.

December 21, 2002:

Bible reference: Proverbs 31:8, 9.

December 25, 2002:

Bible references: Hebrews 2:14-18; Luke 1:41-44.

December 27, 2002:

Bible reference: Isaiah 41:9, 10.

December 28, 2002:

Bible references: John 8:44; 2 Corinthians 11:14;
Matthew 4:10, 11; 28:18.

December 30, 2002:

Bible reference: Psalm 33:18-22.

January 6, 2003:

Bible references: 2 Samuel 14:14; Psalm 33:11;
Isaiah 25:1; Jeremiah 29:11; Romans 11:33; 1
Corinthians 4:5; Revelation 15:3.

Also read Psalm 119:105; Proverbs 3:5-8.

January 9, 2003:

Bible reference: Lamentations 3:22, 23.

January 11, 2003:

Bible references: 1 Corinthians 13:1; Genesis 4:10;
9:4-7; Leviticus 20:1-5; Deuteronomy 21:1-9;
Judges 6:25-32; 1 Kings 18:21; 2 Kings 3:26,

27; Psalms 10:7-10; 106:35-38; Proverbs
1:8-19; 6:16-19; 12:6; Isaiah 59:1-9; Jeremiah
19:4, 5; 32:35; Ezekiel 16:36; Matthew 23:29-
36; Revelation 17:6; 18:24.

January 15, 2003:

Bible references: Job 12:22; 24:13-17; Proverbs
4:18, 19; Daniel 2:22; Mark 4:22; Luke 12:2,
3; John 3:19, 20; Ephesians 5:13; Psalm 49:15;
Isaiah 25:8, 9; Mark 16:6; John 5:24; 10:10,
11; 11:25; Romans 1:4; 1 Corinthians 15:20-
22, 52-58; Hebrews 2:14, 15; 1 Peter 1:3-5; 2
Peter 1:16-21.

January 17, 2003:

Bible references: 1 Samuel 14:6-15; 17:32-50;
Psalms 20:1, 2; 78:1-7; 82:2-4; 94:16; 102:16-
22; Proverbs 3:27-35; Isaiah 49:24, 25; Micah
6:8; Zechariah 8:16, 17; Luke 10:25-37; John
14:12; Romans 13:8-11; Ephesians 5:1-21;
6:10-18; Hebrews 6:10.

January 21, 2003:

Bible references: Job 24:13, 14;
Psalms 57:1-3; 59:1-5.

January 22, 2003:

Bible references: Romans 8:31-39; Genesis 35:18;
Isaiah 9:6, 7; 2 Corinthians 5:8.

Additional observations from Brooke's life

Sarah Weddington, the pro-abortion attorney who won the *Roe v. Wade* case, gave her opening oral argument in Roe before the Supreme Court on December 13, 1971. Brooke was born thirty-one years later on December 13, 2002—a connection I did not discover until eight years after her passing.

Brooke's time in the NICU, her living window to the womb, lasted 40 days from December 13, 2002, to January 21, 2003—a biblically significant timeframe.

The Psalm first chosen for Brooke (Psalm 121) corresponds with her date of passing 1-21-03, January 21st. I first noticed the connection a few days after her death following a vision of Brooke playing chase with her Father in heaven. Verses 7 and 8 of the Psalm have been a great comfort to me.

Brooke went to be with Jesus late in the evening of the 21st about an hour before the 30th observance of the *Roe v. Wade* decision.

also by Joel Patchen

silence can be
deadly...